REAR GARDEN

or

The Cat Who Knew Too Much

by

James Barrie

SEVERUS **SH** HOUSE
YORK, ENGLAND

This edition is published by Severus House publishing

Typeset in 10/11.5pt Garamond

Cover illustration by Robert Clear of London
Cover design by Burak Bakircioglu of Istanbul

ISBN 978-0-9956571-2-0

[TheodoreCat.com]

Contents

Humour and horror are like Siamese Twins
Stephen King

Welcome to God's Own County

She takes a last drag on the cigarette and drops it from her bedroom window, down the gap between the house and the shed, like she has done a thousand times or more, but this time, rather than smouldering out with the rest of the butts, the shed explodes with a bang.

Her dad staggers out. He's on fire. He stands in the middle of the lawn. He flaps his hands against his clothes, trying to put out the flames. He turns and faces the back of his house. He looks up at her bedroom window. 'Hell,' he shouts. 'Hell fire!'

She is 14 years old. She has unicorns and princesses on her curtains, pink and blue. She has grown out of them but her dad has promised her new curtains, yellow ones. She wonders if she'll get the yellow curtains now.

From the bedroom next to hers, she hears her sister scream. She is three years older, about to go off to university.

Then she sees her mum run outside, wet tea towels in her hands. 'Get down on the lawn,' her mum shouts at her dad.

Her dad lies down on the lawn and her mum pushes the wet tea towels against the flames and smouldering clothing. Her dad has stopped screaming and she knows he is dead. His mouth is open; his gums peeled back to show off his yellow teeth.

There is a corpse, with blackened, blistered skin, clothes burnt onto flesh, lying in the middle of the neatly trimmed lawn.

Her mum shakes out one of the tea towels. It is streaked with soot. She lays it over her dad's face.

The tea towel has rolling green hills and winding blue streams on it, and bares the slogan: 'Welcome to God's Own County'.

Constantine Crescent

He had already been incarcerated for several days, or so it seemed. He had no way of knowing for sure. There was no clock on the wall and he had no means to tell the time.

His cell was a carpeted room, five feet by six. A small window without curtains, too high for him to look out of, was set into the wall. The door was shut. There was no way of escape.

He'd been left water and biscuits by his captors. He turned his nose up at the paltry offerings. He paced the room. At least they wanted to keep him alive, he thought, for the time being at least.

After pacing the carpeted floor for what seemed like hours, and relieving himself in a corner of the room, he settled on a makeshift bed in the opposite corner. He soon fell asleep.

When he woke the door was ajar. He stood in front of it for some minutes. It might be a trick.

Then he nudged it further open.

There was a landing, in the same mauve carpet as the room in which he'd been held. As he headed to the top of the stairs, he saw a cat. He turned to face it.

Its fur was silver and white, tinted charcoal. Its eyes were emerald green. Its nose was the brown of cooked liver. Its left ear was curled over, the result of a fight with another cat.

He stared at the cat and the cat stared back. The hair along his spine bristled and his tail stood up straight. The other cat did likewise.

Theodore approached, hissing, and the other cat approached, hissing back at him. It was quite a formidable foe, Theodore thought, and quite a handsome specimen.

It was him after all, he realised, as he came nose to nose with his reflection. He glanced behind the mirror, leaning against the landing wall, just to make sure. He raised his tail and carried on along the landing.

He examined the mauve pile of the carpet; noted the strange odours left by previous occupants, the dark stains, the strange brown sticky patches. Then he padded downstairs to investigate this new domain further.

In the kitchen he discovered his water bowl and a fresh bowl of cat biscuits in the corner. He ate several. They tasted no different to how they had tasted that morning, back at his old home in Clementhorpe. At least somethings did not change, he thought, approaching the back door.

There was no cat flap. He stared for a moment at the lack of an opening in the door, his tail raised high. He miaowed.

'You're not going anywhere, Theo,' Emily said. 'You've a litter tray over there.'

Theodore looked over at the covered tray in the corner. He swished his tail from side to side. For Bastet's sake, he swore under his breath, invoking the name of the Cat Goddess. How was he to maintain his dignity while having to relieve himself in a plastic tray with a see-through flap? How would a human like it?

'It's only for a couple of weeks,' Emily said, arms folded across her chest and shaking her head.

Emily's attention was then drawn to the litter tray and its contents. 'Jonathan,' she said. 'You bought the wrong type of litter…'

4

'The wrong type?' Jonathan said, looking up from his mobile phone. 'I just bought the cheapest one.'

'I can see that,' Emily said. 'It turns to sludge.'

Theodore miaowed in agreement.

'Well, I'm not going out again to buy more litter. He can make do with what he's got for now... Next time I'll know. How long do we need to keep the litter tray inside anyway?'

'Just until Theo knows where his new home is,' Emily said.

'And how long will that be?'

'A fortnight,' Emily said. 'He's not going out before then. He's got to get used to his new home. Two weeks... That's what they say. Then we'll need to butter his paws...'

Theodore stared up at her, his eyes wide in disbelief. Buttering paws? What sort of barbaric nonsense was this?

'It will fly by,' Emily said, reading his feline mind, before bending down to stroke his head. 'I'm going to unpack some more boxes,' she said. 'They're not going to unpack themselves.'

Some minutes later Jonathan, still on his mobile, watched as Emily struggled into the kitchen with a box.

'This one weighs a tonne... What's in it?' she said. 'Rocks?'

'That'll be my fossil collection,' Jonathan said. 'I was going to put them in the front room.'

'We're not having rocks in the front room,' Emily said. 'They can go in the garden. You can make a rockery with them.'

'But they're valuable,' Jonathan protested. 'They took me years to collect.'

Emily opened the kitchen door. 'I think rocks belong in the garden,' she said.

She placed the box outside the kitchen door and returned inside.

There was a knock at the front door and Emily went to answer it.

Theodore followed at her heels. It may be an opportunity to gain a few minutes of freedom, he thought.

'I'm your neighbour,' a man with shaggy grey hair under a red cap said. 'I brought round a little house-warming present.'

'Oh, thank you,' Emily said, opening the door a little further to take the punnet of red tomatoes. 'They look nice and ripe.'

Aware that Theodore was standing behind her, brushing up against her bare calves, she held the door open only enough to accept the house-warming present.

'My cat,' she explained, 'I can't let him out.'

'What was that?' her new neighbour said. 'I'm a bit hard of hearing.'

'My cat,' Emily said loudly. 'I don't want him to get out.'

'Good,' her new neighbour said. 'They can make an awful mess.'

'Mess?'

'In gardens. You see, I've got green fingers and I'd prefer to keep them that way.'

He opened his mouth and laughed showing off a large gap between his middle teeth.

Emily looked down at the blood red tomatoes in the little green box and then back at her grinning new neighbour.

'They're very red,' she said, 'the tomatoes.'

'Yes,' the grey-haired man replied, nodding his head, still smiling. 'It's the bone meal. I make my own bone meal.'

'I see,' Emily said. 'How quaint…'

The man laughed.

Emily felt Theodore's fur once more, against the backs of her bare calves, and felt her skin begin to prickle. She inched the front door closed.

'The cat,' she said. 'I don't want him to get out.'

'No, he's best kept indoors,' the man said. 'Like I said… Well, I need to be on my way. Errands!'

'Well, thank you for the tomatoes,' Emily said.

'It's Walter,' the man said. 'But everyone calls me Wally.'

'Well, nice to meet you, erm… Wally. And thank you again for the tomatoes. We can have them with our dinner.'

'The pleasure is all mine… Sorry, I didn't catch your name.'

'Emily,' said Emily.

'A pleasure indeed,' said Wally.

'My boyfriend's in the kitchen,' Emily added, and then pushed the door to.

It was evident that Wally didn't like cats. He was probably a mouse in a past life, thought Theodore, staring at the back of the front door.

He stayed staring at the front door for a long minute. It was only April but his new neighbour had already managed to grow his own tomatoes. Theodore wasn't too familiar with horticulture having spent his youth in the backyards and cobbled alleys of Clementhorpe, but something did not seem right.

So far April had been a bipolar month – swinging between sunny days to others overcast with icy showers of rain. *Was it possible to grow ripe tomatoes in April?*

He turned round.

On the vestibule door, Emily had hung a small sign.

A
HOUSE
IS NOT A
HOME
WITHOUT A
CAT

He pondered the words for a moment and then padded into the front room and, from up on the windowsill, he took in the street.

Constantine Crescent is a tree-lined street built by the Quakers mainly in the early 1920s, though construction had started in 1914 before being disrupted by the First World War. It is horse-shoe shaped, beginning and ending on York Street, Acomb – York's largest residential suburb.

The houses are a mixture of detached and semi-detached, with a few bungalows thrown in. Not one house on the street is the same as another. The Quakers understood that people are different and they like their houses to be different too. The trees that line the grassed verges are all lime. They had yet to sprout their waxy leaves.

Many of the houses had net curtains across their windows. Theodore sensed many eyes looking back at him from behind their veiled screens. A net curtain twitched from behind a display of Pampas Grass from the house in front.

Suburbia…, thought Theodore. How boring.

Then he noticed his new neighbour, Wally, mounting his bicycle and launching himself into the road; off on his errands, Theodore presumed, the bottom of his brown trousers tucked into his brown socks.

As Wally passed by, he turned and waved at Theodore, smiling his gappy smile. The world slowed down for a moment. Theodore blinked and then Wally was gone.

Then along the street, from the other direction, an ice cream van approached. It was driven by a fat, balding man, who toted a fat cigar. As it neared, the chimes played *The Funeral March of a Marionette*.

I make my own bone meal, Wally had said. Theodore's brow furrowed. What was bone meal made out of? he asked himself.

Bones, he answered. Whose or what's bones?

The hair along his spine began to bristle.

Perhaps he made his bone meal out of cats' bones…

Wally's Big Mouth

Later, as Emily and Jonathan ate their chicken dinner, Theodore sat below the table. Emily had been known to drop the odd scrap on the floor in the past. That was before she had moved in together with Jonathan though. The dynamics had evidently changed.

He loitered hopefully, flicking his tail against Emily's bare calves from time to time to make sure she knew he was there, waiting.

Neither Emily nor Jonathan spoke while they ate. They had hoped to move into the house on Constantine Crescent before Christmas but it was almost Easter by the time they finally moved in.

The last few months their lives had been in suspended animation; their possessions in boxes in their respective homes, caught between two worlds with little to talk about apart from the upcoming move. So it was with a sense of relief that they had finally signed the papers in the solicitor's office, had a moving date confirmed, booked the removal company and, with a big sigh of relief, it was done.

As anyone who has listened to others talk about moving house knows, it is only interesting to those who are actually doing the moving, so it was also a huge relief to those who knew Emily and Jonathan that they had finally moved in.

Jonathan was chewing on a chicken wing. 'The Chinese believe the wing to be the best part of the chicken,' he said.

'I like best those little bits from underneath,' said Emily.

'The oysters?' Jonathan said.

'Is that they're called?'

'That's what I call them.' Jonathan took some salad from a bowl in the middle of the table. 'Did you use the tomatoes our new neighbour brought round?' he asked.

'Yes, why?' Emily said. 'They looked very ripe. I thought we should use them straightaway.'

'They taste a bit beefy.'

'Beefy?' Emily took a slice of tomato and chewed on it. 'Perhaps they're beef tomatoes,' she said.

'Not sure I've had *beef* tomatoes before,' he said.

'He said something about making his own bone meal.'

They ate in silence for a minute, pondering the significance of making your own bone meal.

'I'm in Derbyshire tomorrow,' Jonathan said, changing the subject. 'Looking for sinkholes...'

'Sinkholes?' Emily said, picking up a leg and taking a bite.

Jonathan explained that the area was prone to limestone dissolution.

'Oh, sinkholes,' Emily said, licking her greasy fingers. An image of a field with buried kitchen sinks scattered around came to her mind.

'A nice walk in the countryside and being paid for it,' Jonathan went on. 'It doesn't get better than that.'

'Well, just be careful,' Emily said.

'Of what?'

'The sinkholes, stupid. You might trip up in one.'

Jonathan laughed. 'I'll be fine,' he said.

Theodore looked at the bare floorboards. Not a scrap of chicken. He flicked his tail against Emily's bare calf, aiming the tip at the back of her knee.

Emily's hand appeared below the table. She flicked the back of her fingers against his side. 'You be patient! You'll get some later…' she said.

Theodore exited from beneath the table. He headed into the hallway and then made his way upstairs. He added his own scent as he went, rubbing himself against the steps. It wouldn't be too long before his own smell dominated the new house.

On the upstairs landing he paused. There were three bedrooms and a bathroom. The front bedroom was Emily and Jonathan's. One of the back bedrooms was crammed with cardboard boxes, waiting to be unpacked. The other back bedroom he knew too well; he had spent half the day locked in it and had no desire to return. So he made his way into the room filled with cardboard boxes and navigated his way through this temporary landscape.

From the windowsill he took in the garden below.

His previous house had just a concrete yard with one raised bed against the boundary wall. He now looked out across the lawn, to the islands of daffodils and the overgrown rockery beyond. There were long grasses and euphorbia, a rhododendron and other small shrubs. Behind the plants and shrubs, there was a hedge: part privet, part hawthorn. Through a gap at the bottom of the hedge, a ginger head appeared.

The head looked from side to side, and then a ginger cat emerged. Theodore miaowed at the glass but the ginger cat did not hear, or chose to ignore him.

Hamish strutted between the shrubs. He had got used to the garden being part of his territory, the previous occupant having moved out some months before. He looked up at Theodore. He widened his green eyes, as if to say: 'What are you going to do about it?'

Then he raised his rear end and sprayed the rhododendron, before making his way through a cluster of daffodils and padding across Theodore's lawn.

Once Hamish had returned through the gap in the hedge, Theodore turned his attention to the house next door.

He spied the greenhouse, where he assumed the tomatoes had come from, though there was little sign of anything green inside. Beside the greenhouse, there was a shed, which backed onto a hedge that formed the boundary with the house behind. On top of the shed was a little pole with a little flag. A white rose on a pastel blue background: the flag of Yorkshire.

On the other side of the hedge, there was another shed. This one had the blue and white cross of St Andrew. Theodore understood that the humans were showing their territorial affiliations, as cats marked their territory by spraying.

Theodore's father was a Scottish Fold and his mother a Ragdoll, born and bred in Yorkshire. He had no qualms about his heritage. He was where he was now. Humans were a different kettle of fish, he realised, though wondered what kettles and fish had to do with questions of national identity. He blinked his eyes. He was thinking too much, too much into human nature. Perhaps a bit more interbreeding is what's required, he concluded.

Then, from down below, he heard a woman call: 'Wally! Time for tea...'

There was no response from the shed.

The woman walked to the edge of the lawn, before shouting across, 'Wally! Wally!'

Wally finally emerged from his shed, walked across the lawn, along a well-trodden path.

To the rear of the house, there was a conservatory. The conservatory was roofed in opaque plastic sheeting. Theodore made out a table and chairs, the table set for two.

'What are we having, Marje?' Wally said.

'Quiche,' Marjorie said. 'And salad.'

'What kind of quiche?' said Wally.

'Hamon.'

'Ah, ham and salmon,' Wally said. 'You know that's one of my favourites.'

'I know,' said Marjorie with a smile.

They sat down at the table, and Wally poured them both mugs of tea from the pot. He added salad to his plate.

'That reminds me,' he said with a grin. 'I went round and met our new neighbours today. Introduced myself, you know.'

'Oh, yes,' Marjorie said. 'How are they?'

'They seem nice enough. A young couple... I only met her. Well, I gave her some of those tomatoes...'

Wally began to laugh. He threw back his head, showing his gappy grin.

'What's so funny?' Marjorie said.

Wally stopped laughing for long enough to tell Marjorie that he had told the young woman next door that he made his own bone meal.

'Made your own bone meal?' Marjorie said. 'Whatever must they be thinking? You great Wally!'

Wally spluttered on a piece of celery. He coughed, and then swallowed loudly. He took a drink of tea.

Marjorie tutted. 'Why, they probably think you're here now, grinding up bones in your shed...'

Wally grinned, his cheeks red.

Marjorie shook her head. 'You silly old thing...'

'I was only joking.'

'That big mouth of yours,' Marjorie said, 'is going to get you into trouble one of these days!' She wagged a knowing finger at her husband. 'Mark my words.'

14

The Watcher & the Watched

The next day Jonathan fell down a sinkhole in Derbyshire and fractured the navicular bone in his left foot. He was provided with an aircast boot (a large grey, plastic moon boot), and painkillers, Naproyn and Tylenol, and told that he would have to keep the boot on for at least four weeks. If he didn't, he might walk with a limp for the rest of his life, he'd been warned.

'I'm going to be laid up for weeks,' he complained from the sofa, his booted foot propped up on a little coffee table.

'I did warn you,' Emily pointed out, 'about those sinkholes.'

'I'm not going to be able to drive or anything.'

Emily was removing DVDs from a cardboard box and stacking them on a shelf below the television. 'How convenient,' she said under her breath.

'I won't be able to do anything but sit here,' Jonathan went on.

'You're not going to be much use to anyone,' Emily said irritably. 'Just let me do everything…'

'What am I going to do for four weeks? We don't even have Sky installed.'

Emily turned and said, 'You could watch some of these DVDs.'

She removed from the shelf a box set of Alfred Hitchcock films that she had just put there. 'You could start with these,' she said.

'Hitchcock?'

'Why not? They're classics.'

'I could give them a go,' Jonathan said. 'I'm going to be stuck here for weeks. If I put pressure on my foot, I could end up with a limp for the rest of my life.'

'Well, at least you've got Theodore. You can keep each other company and watch Hitchcock together. He always used to sit and watch Columbo with me. I think he liked Columbo...'

Jonathan stroked Theodore, who was sitting on the sofa beside him.

Theodore eyed Jonathan. I'm going to be out of here before you, he thought, and jumped down onto the floor and approached the French windows. He spotted ginger Hamish squatting down beside the rhododendron. He miaowed out at the garden.

Hamish finished his business. The ginger cat made a cursory inspection and then sauntered back to his own home, without bothering to cover.

Jonathan was wearing a dressing gown over an old t-shirt. On his right foot he wore an old rugby sock, dark blue and light blue hoops. On his left foot he wore the grey plastic boot.

He looked out of the French windows.

The house directly behind was at a higher level, so that from Jonathan's position on the sofa he could see over the top of the back hedge and into the two first-floor bedroom windows that faced him.

He saw a middle-aged woman in one window, the one on the right. Her face was heavily made up, large rimmed glasses on her face and a blond wig on her head, slightly dishevelled. The curtains were partly drawn and the light from a television flickered against the yellow and brown floral pattern.

The woman looked out from the window, and Jonathan watched as she raised a bottle and took a swig from it.

16

In the next window a younger woman in her twenties, probably the daughter, Jonathan guessed, was smoking a cigarette. She was sucking on the cigarette and then blowing the smoke up and out of the window. Jonathan realised she must be kneeling up on her bed. The room was lit up from a lamp so her figure was outlined from behind. As his eyes focussed on the woman, he realised that she was wearing only a black bra that contrasted against the pinkish white of her skin.

Jonathan noted that she was generously proportioned. If he were in the field, he would have described them in geological terms as 'Off white/cream, well-rounded cobbles of alabaster…'

He glanced back at the other window. The older woman took another swig from her bottle and then adjusted her wig.

On the other sofa, perpendicular to the one Jonathan was sitting on, and facing the television, Emily sat, absorbed in some US crime drama. She was wearing a onesie she had got for Christmas, a giant pink rabbit, though she didn't have the hood over her head.

Jonathan looked at the television but soon his attention was drawn again to the French windows and the house behind. He watched as the younger woman, the daughter, dropped her cigarette from the top of the window and then pulled the curtains slowly together. Her body was perfectly outlined against the pink and blue of the curtains.

Then the curtains parted an inch in the middle and Jonathan knew that she was peering out. Peering back at him.

He adjusted his dressing gown, pulling it down below his knees.

He was no longer the watcher but the watched.

He looked over at Emily, still staring at the television and nibbling on minty Matchmakers.

He looked back at the window behind; the curtains were closed. 'We really need to get some curtains to go over the French windows,' he said.

'Full height curtains,' Emily said, 'are going to cost a fortune.'

'Maybe some sheets,' Jonathan said. 'Just for the time being.'

'There is no way we are putting sheets up.'

'It's just that,' Jonathan said, 'we are a bit overlooked.'

Emily glared across at Jonathan; then said, 'Where's Theo got to?'

Theodore was in the upstairs bedroom.

He looked out from the windowsill. He had watched the young woman smoke her cigarette through the window. He had seen her drop the lit cigarette onto the paving stones below the window. He had watched as the red glow from the cigarette end had grown smaller and smaller and finally gone out.

He heard a rat-a-tat from the garden to his right.

This garden was bigger and belonged to a long, low-slung bungalow. An extension took up the entire rear.

A grey-haired man in a dressing gown and mirrored glasses was standing in the doorway of the conservatory, shaking a box of dog biscuits. 'Lucy! Lucy!' he called. 'Are you there, Lucy?'

Theodore noticed some movement in the bungalow's garden and then a Labrador appeared in the yellow light cast by the conservatory, the reflective bands on its harness catching the light.

Lucy approached the man, wagging her tail, and the man in dark glasses attached a lead to the dog's harness. After the dog had led its owner back inside, the blind man locked the doors and retreated inside his house for the night, turning on the lights out of habit rather than need.

Theodore looked over the top of the bungalow. He made out the steeple of a church, St Stephen's, surrounded by beeches, oaks and elms. Theodore blinked as the dying light disappeared behind the church and then jumped down from the windowsill.

Downstairs Jonathan was still sitting on the sofa. His booted broken foot was propped up on the coffee table in front of him; his head was sunk back into a cushion. His mouth was open and he was snoring.

Theodore looked over at the French windows and the garden beyond, now in darkness.

The television had been left on. There was a 1980s' film on called *Body Double*.

Theodore watched as Holly Body, played by Melanie Griffith, gets drilled to death on the floor of her apartment, while Jake Scully, played by Craig Wasson, looks on helplessly from his own apartment window.

The Morning Rush

The next morning Emily left for work at quarter past seven. Before she left, she reminded Jonathan that her mother was going to pop round with some lunch for him.

'Don't get into mischief while I'm gone,' Emily called from the hallway, putting on her coat.

'That's not very likely, is it?' Jonathan called back from the sofa.

'And make sure Theo doesn't get out,' Emily called, opening the front door.

'I'll do my best,' Jonathan shouted, only to be answered by the front door shutting behind her.

Emily almost tripped over her neighbour Sam, who was bent down picking up a small dog turd from the footpath.

Sam held the turd in a little blue bag at arm's length. In her other hand she gripped a lead that was attached to a fat Chihuahua, its body the size and shape of a melon.

'I'm Sam. I'd shake your hand but, as you can see, they are both fully occupied.'

'I don't know how you can do that,' Emily said, staring at the little blue bag. 'First thing in the morning.'

'You can't leave it there,' Sam said. 'Not with the neighbourhood gestapo looking on... I'd be reported to the Council. Then firing squad at dawn.'

'I couldn't do it,' Emily said. 'I'm a cat person. Cat people don't have to pick up poo.'

'Well, I'm a dog person,' Sam said, 'and it's the price we have to pay… And this is Charlie.'

Emily looked down at the little dog. It was whipping its tail from side to side, and showing its little teeth in a fierce grin.

'Hello Charlie… I'm Emily. My cat is bigger than you.'

She bent down and was about to pat the dog on the head but Charlie, perhaps in his excitement, squatted down again and let out a sliver of diarrhoea.

Sam grimaced. 'He's got such a sensitive tummy.'

'I need to get going,' Emily said, making her way past Sam and the still squatting Chihuahua to her car. 'I'm running late…'

'I'll wash it away later,' Sam called after her, squinting down at the brown streak on the pavement.

Theodore watched from the bay window of the front room. He looked at the little blue bag and then the mess on the footpath. He watched as Emily's car made its way down the street, still in second gear.

Cat People and Dog People? He closed his eyes and imagined a world populated by humanoid cats and humanoid dogs.

When he opened his eyes again, he saw people dashing by on their way to work. Mums and dads pushed prams and pushchairs with one hand, clasping handbags or briefcases in the other. Children were bundled or ordered into cars, depending on their age, only to join the queue of traffic on York Road. Cyclists with determined faces and crust in the corner of their eyes sped past. Fashionable men strode past in brown shoes and tight trousers, their faces adorned with trimmed bushy beards. Young children were dragged along by parents who feared they would be late for work. A man who had had a stroke walked lopsidedly past, on his way for the newspaper.

Then a woman in purple emerged from the house opposite. 'What a lovely morning!' she called over to Sam and Charlie, who were returning along the street.

'Yes, isn't it, Linda?' Sam called back. Charlie the Chihuahua strained at his lead, desperate to be let off.

'Such a shame he can't be let off his lead,' Linda said, crossing the road towards Sam and Charlie.

'He'd run away,' Sam said. 'I couldn't bear to lose my Charlie.'

'I'm on my way to yoga with laughter,' Linda said. 'It's very therapeutic... You should try it. Don't want to be late!' She hurried on down the street.

Charlie strained at his lead, flicking his little tail from side to side, not wanting his walk to end. He knew that the rest of the day he would be shut in by himself.

Then a man in a suit appeared and said, 'Hurry up, Sam. You know I have a breakfast meeting. I really need to get going.'

He didn't really. He was meeting his personal assistant for some pre-office personal assistance.

'I know, Steve,' Sam said. 'I'll just be a minute... Tidying up after Charlie, you know.' She held the little blue bag in the air.

'Just hurry up,' Steve said. 'I really don't have the time.'

'Just give me a minute.' Sam yanked the Chihuahua around and began dragging him back towards her house.

Ten minutes later Steve was sitting in his car, a white Audi, blowing his horn. Steve enjoyed blowing his horn.

He blew his horn until several minutes later his wife, who had been a hairdresser in Harrogate before she met Steve in a bar in York, came out of the house.

She opened the car door. 'What's the big hurry anyway?' she said.

'I told you... I have a breakfast meeting,' Steve almost shouted. 'And now I am already late.'

He knew that if he missed his pre-office appointment he would be frustrated and bad-tempered the rest of the day.

'Well, Charlie had to go to the loo, didn't he? Wouldn't want him having an accident in the house while we were out, would we?'

'No, we wouldn't,' Steve said. 'That carpet cost two thousand quid.'

'You don't always have to bring up what things cost all the time,' Sam said, still not getting into the car. 'Have a little decorum.'

'I'm going to be late,' Steve shouted. 'Because I have to drive you to your spa. Why can't you learn to drive for heaven's sake.'

'You know I don't drive, darling,' Sam said and then slid into the Audi.

As soon as the passenger door closed, Steve sped off down the street, within seconds exceeding the twenty mile an hour limit.

All this rushing about, thought Theodore. You need to set the pace for the long haul. No point rushing towards death; it'll only come looking for you.

He stretched his body, arched his back, and then settled onto his haunches. It was definitely time for a nap.

Soup Selection

Theodore woke midmorning.

A coach had pulled up further along the street and scores of Chinese tourists were getting out. Most of the tourists were clutching phones and cameras. They wandered up and down the suburban street, stopping in front of houses and taking photos of each other. Some had selfie sticks and took photos of themselves standing in the street. Others entered people's gardens and took more photos. Curtains up and down the street twitched.

I supposed you have to come from a country with a population of over a billion to appreciate the mundanity of suburbia, thought Theodore.

Twenty minutes later, the Chinese tourists got back on their coach and departed for a discount retail unit on the outskirts of York. The street was quiet once more, as though they had never been.

Theodore wandered into the lounge.

Jonathan was sitting on the sofa, his foot still propped on the little coffee table. He had spent most of the morning playing random strangers at Scrabble. He was now waiting for fifteen people to take their turns.

The remote controls were laid in a row on the arm of the sofa. 'Shall we watch *Rear Window*?' he asked Theodore, patting the empty seat next to him.

Theodore jumped up onto the sofa next to Jonathan.

'I take it that's a yes,' Jonathan said, turning the DVD player on.

Theodore settled down against Jonathan's side, and together they stared at the Greenwich Village scene.

Jonathan had not attempted to go to bed the night before. Instead, aided by a bottle of wine, he had fallen asleep where he was sitting while watching *Body Double*.

He'd woken at four in the morning and couldn't get back to sleep. He retrieved a book, *The Glacial Geology of Holderness and The Vale of York* by Sidney Melmore, coincidentally a former resident of Acomb, thinking it would help him to get back to sleep, but twenty pages later, he noticed the sky begin to lighten and the birds in full song.

On the screen James Stewart said into the telephone: 'He killed a dog last night because the dog was scratching around in the garden. You know why? Because he had something buried in that garden…'

Theodore looked over at Jonathan; the human looked deep in thought. He continued to watch the Hitchcock film, and when it had finished and the DVD returned to the start menu, he got down from the sofa. Jonathan had fallen asleep.

Theodore wandered into the kitchen and inspected his bowls. He went to the corner where the litter box was but then remembered that Jonathan had bought the wrong type of litter.

He went back into the lounge and approached the French windows. He peered out into the garden.

Hamish, the ginger tom, was sitting in the middle of the lawn. The hairs along Theodore's spine stood on end. Hamish caught his stare and held it.

Had there not been a pane of glass between them, Theodore would have seen off the intruder.

Soon as I'm out of here, he growled to himself, we'll see whose garden it is…

He was sitting on a Turkish rug that Jonathan had contributed to the house.

Jonathan had had the rug since his teenage years. It had been under his feet in his bedroom in Market Weighton, where he had lived with his parents. It had accompanied him to university in Leeds, where it had adorned his room at Bodington Hall, and then two attic rooms in Headingley. Before he had moved in with Emily, it had been in his front room in the little terraced house he had rented in South Bank, York.

Theodore had noticed a fine fuzz of black hairs coating the carpet. He sniffed the rug and smelled another cat: Jonathan's former cat, Edward. Theodore had had enough of other cats. He squatted down on the rug.

Once he'd finished, he made his way upstairs and settled on the windowsill in the back bedroom. The window was open a couple of inches, but not wide enough for Theodore to fit through.

Apart from the birds' tweeting, there were no other noises. Most grown-ups were at work, children at school, cats napping the day away. This was as it should be. Jonathan had no right to be at home, disturbing his daytime peace. There was a limit to the hours Theodore could spend in the company of humans.

Then, in the house behind, Theodore noticed the younger woman warming soup in the kitchen.

Ellen was making soup for lunch. She lived with and cared for her mum Tessa. It was just the two of them; her father Colin had died ten years ago, and her sister Penny had moved away, to university in Bristol, and then stayed on and got a job in that city.

Ellen brought the soup to a gentle simmer. She poured some into a bowl, which she placed onto an orange plastic tray and carried it upstairs.

A minute later, Theodore saw Ellen enter the back bedroom. Her mother was sitting up in bed. A television in the corner of the bedroom was turned on to a shopping channel.

A Shih Tzu, Sandy, yapped, jumped down from the bed and ran through the open door and down the stairs.

'It's lunchtime, mum,' Ellen said.

'Is it?' Tessa said, sitting up. 'Already?'

Ellen sniffed the air. 'Have you been drinking already?'

'No, of course not,' Tessa said. 'It's only just lunchtime... Now, where's Sandy?'

'He went downstairs,' Ellen said. 'He might need to go out.'

Theodore could hear the dog yapping, out of sight.

Ellen placed the tray in front of her mother.

'What is it?'

'Curried parsnip.'

'Curried parsnip? But I don't like curried parsnip.'

'But mum,' Ellen said, 'it's your favourite.'

'Now I'm sure I would remember if it were my favourite, wouldn't I?'

She pushed back her glasses with her forefinger.

'Well, yes, mum,' Ellen said. 'You would remember.'

'I don't like curried parsnip,' Tessa said, her voice raised. 'In fact I hate curried parsnip soup. Whoever heard of such a thing? Curried parsnips!'

'But you haven't tried it.'

'I'm not going to eat that muck,' she said. 'It stinks.'

Ellen reached over and lifted the tray from the duvet, before her mother could overturn it. 'I can get you something else,' Ellen offered. 'How about chicken? Chicken soup. You like chicken soup.'

'Yes, I like chicken soup.'

Ellen carried the tray to the door. 'I won't be long,' she said. 'I'll make you some nice chicken soup.'

'Where's Sandy,' Tessa asked.

'He just went downstairs. He probably needed to go out.'

'Well, go and let him out if he needs to go,' Tessa said.

Ellen went downstairs and Tessa turned and faced the window. She looked down into the garden to see if she could see Sandy.

Her lips were painted red, smudged across her lower face. Her blonde wig was again at an angle. She peered down into the garden. She glanced back at her bedroom door and then retrieved a bottle of Lambrini from the gap between her bed and the wall. Theodore watched as she took a swig of sparkling perry. He noticed her wedding ring, set with diamonds, sparkling in the light.

Ellen was back downstairs in the kitchen. She opened the back door and let Sandy out into the overgrown garden, where the dog defecated on the lawn. The small heap joined the hundreds of others.

Ellen poured the bowl of curried parsnip soup down the sink. She opened a cupboard and took out another can of soup, checked the flavour and then put it in a clean saucepan. While the soup was warming, she poured the remainder of the curried parsnip soup into a bowl, and sat down at the kitchen table and ate it, her face bent over the bowl.

From downstairs in his own home, Theodore heard Jonathan shouting his name. He remembered what he had done to his rug and thought it best to stay put in the back bedroom. There was no way Jonathan could make it upstairs. He closed his ears to the shouts and curses coming from downstairs. The sun had come out and he felt it warming his fur.

Later, he heard a familiar voice, now a little slurred. 'But I don't like chicken soup.'

He opened his eyes, and in the house opposite he saw that Tessa had a new bowl of soup in front of her.

'Well, what soup do you like?' Ellen's voice now had an edge of desperation.

'Mushroom,' Tessa said. 'I like mushroom soup. Mushroom soup is my favourite.'

'All right,' Ellen said, picking the tray back up from the bed. 'I'll be back in a few minutes... With a bowl of mushroom soup.' She left the room but didn't return to the kitchen.

A minute later she re-entered her mother's bedroom. 'Here mum,' she said, 'I've brought you some lovely mushroom soup.'

She placed the tray back down on the bed covers in front of her mother.

'Mushroom soup,' Tessa said. 'Yes, I do like a bowl of mushroom soup.'

'I know you do,' Ellen said. 'Now I'd better be getting on.'

'Where's Sandy?'

'He's outside.'

'Well, let him in.'

Ellen left the room and a minute later was back downstairs. She let Sandy back in and then sat at the dining table and lit a cigarette.

Theodore wondered about the conversation he had overheard regarding Tessa's preference for soups. He was still wondering when there was a knocking at his own front door.

He heard Jonathan call out, 'Come in... I'm in the lounge.'

Theodore jumped down from the windowsill and went to the top of the stairs.

'Oh dear,' Emily's mother, Trish, said. 'Whatever is that smell? Have you had an accident, Jonathan?'

'I haven't had an accident,' Jonathan said. 'Theodore has done something on the rug.'

Trish went into the lounge, her hand across her mouth and nose. 'Well, I'd better get some detergent and some gloves on,' she said and coughed into her palm. 'I don't know how you can bear it in here. You don't even have a window open.' She crossed the lounge and opened a window. 'There. That's a bit better,' she said, coughing once more.

'Thank you,' Jonathan said.

'Now let me find some rubber gloves,' Trish said. 'We'll soon have this cleaned up.'

Once Trish had gone into the kitchen, Theodore wandered in.

He took up position under the dining table, behind Jonathan. He stared up at the open window. The window was over another two-seater sofa, placed perpendicular to the one on which Jonathan was sitting. From the back of the sofa, it was a simple step up onto the window sill. Then there was a three foot jump up to the wide open window. Then a drop of no more than six feet on the other side, down to the ground below... To the Outside World. This was his opportunity.

He dashed forward, past Jonathan, towards the open window.

Going to the Dogs

'Trish!' Jonathan shouted.

Trish hurried into the lounge, yellow, suddy rubber gloves on her hands. 'Whatever is it now?'

'It's Theodore,' Jonathan said. 'He's got out of the window. He's not supposed to be let out...'

Trish crossed to the French windows and saw her daughter's large fluffy grey cat dart across the lawn and head towards the hedge at the back of the garden.

'Oh dear,' she said. 'These windows could really do with a clean.'

She wiped her forefinger across the glass.

'Both inside and out...' she said and shook her head.

Theodore made for the gap in the hedge. Seconds later he was through it and into the garden behind. There was a yapping from the house and clashing of paws against a door. He was in Shih Tzu territory.

He stood rigid in the middle of the lawn, among a minefield of dog shit. At least he's locked in, he thought. He can't get at me.

Then the kitchen door swung open and the little dog came rushing out, yapping. Straight at him.

Theodore just managed to make it to the boundary hedge, find a gap and dive through to the next garden.

Sandy the Shih Tzu yapped from behind, unable to squeeze through the hawthorn hedge.

Theodore took in his new surroundings. He was standing in a patch of soil dotted with young plants. The vegetable patch occupied most of the back garden

31

apart from a large shed to his left. There was a narrow strip of lawn, and then a patio that went up to the back of the house. A man with a power spray was jetting down the flagstones.

It is said that many people resemble their dogs, or their dogs resemble them. Well, Stuart resembled his cat Hamish. He had ginger hair cropped short; the ginger hair continued across most of his face as stubble, and his eyes were green and bright.

Stuart turned and noticed the large grey fluffy cat in his vegetable patch. He raised his power spray and aimed the jet at Theodore.

'We come here with no peaceful intent, but ready for battle,' Stuart cried, quoting William Wallace, 'determined to avenge our wrongs and set our country free. Let your masters come and attack us: we are ready to meet them beard to beard!'

From behind Theodore, Sandy yapped. From in front a jet of water hit him. He turned to the side, and headed for another hedge. He was through it and up the vertical face of a shed, Wally's shed. For a moment he was relieved to feel the warm felt of the shed roof beneath his paws. Then water lashed the wooden wall of the shed below him.

'I have brought you to the ring, now see if you can dance,' Stuart cried, aiming the jet at him once more, arching it over the shed roof.

'What's going on here?' Wally shouted across the top of the hedge.

'That cat was in my tattie patch,' Stuart said, red in the face. 'I was defending my territory.'

'Well, he's not in your territory now,' Wally said, burring his r's to mimic Stuart's pronounced roll. 'He's on my shed, and I say he can stay up there.'

'We'll see about that,' Stuart said, sending another arc of water over the shed roof.

'Don't you get your bagpipes in a twist, you silly Scottish haggis!'

Stuart turned redder in the face.

'You think you can tell me what to do on my own land? Take that, English pig!'

He pointed his jet spray at Wally, catching him in the face.

'Put that spray down,' Trish shouted from over the hedge. 'That's my daughter's cat up there.'

Stuart lowered his power spray and released his grip. 'He was in my tattie patch,' he shouted across at her.

'That's no reason to soak him. He's absolutely sodden,' Trish called back. 'If he comes down with cat flu, you'll be paying the vet's bills.'

'I won't be paying anything of the sort.'

'We'll see about that!'

From the felt roof of the shed, Theodore took in the scene. There was Stuart, jet washer in hand, standing in the middle of his potato patch. Wally standing by his shed, wiping water from his face. Then there was Trish, still in rubber gloves, pointing an accusing yellow finger at Stuart from the corner of his garden. He looked over at the house behind his own. Sandy the Shih Tzu was yapping from behind the hedge, out of sight.

There was a dull crack and Theodore looked up at Tessa's bedroom window.

While the two men and Trish bickered over the hedges, Theodore saw Ellen in Tessa's bedroom. Chicken soup slid slowly down the bedroom wall across daisy-patterned wallpaper. Ellen was on her knees, picking up pieces of broken porcelain. He couldn't see Tessa but he could hear her.

'It was chicken,' Tessa was saying. 'You gave me chicken soup. You know I don't like chicken soup. It's carcass scrapings.'

'It was mushroom, mum,' Ellen said.

'Don't you mum me. I know your game,' Tessa said. 'You can't wait for me to pop my clogs; then you'll get the house. That's why you're hanging around, isn't it? Well, just you wait. You've got another thing coming. If only your dad was around to see it!'

'I never thought anything of the sort,' Ellen said.

'Well, I've been to see Mr Philby,' Tessa said. 'If anything happens to me, everything will go to the dogs' home, do you hear? The house! His stamps! Everything! Do you understand?'

'Yes, mum,' Ellen said, a stammer in her voice. 'I understand.'

'Going to the dogs! Tessa screamed. 'Going to the DOGS!'

'Please calm down,' Ellen said.

'Don't tell me to calm down,' Tessa shrieked. 'GOING TO THE DOGS!'

From below him Theodore heard Trish shout, 'You don't go near my daughter's cat ever again!'

He looked down at the people squabbling over the hedge. He looked back at his own house. Jonathan was standing in the French windows, holding himself up with his crutches.

Then he looked back over at Tessa's bedroom window.

Ellen was now standing in front of the window, looking down at the scene below. They maintained eye contact for a few seconds. Then Ellen snapped the curtains closed. They had sunflowers on them, yellow and brown.

A moment later Theodore jumped down from the shed roof, scrabbled through the bottom of the hedge, into his own garden and let himself be grabbed up by Trish.

34

A Nation of Peeping Toms

When Emily got back from work, her mother had gone, leaving a tin-foiled dish of lasagne in the fridge for their dinner.

'How's your day been?' she asked Jonathan, before noticing that Theodore was sitting in front of the open French windows, his legs crossed in front of him, looking out at the garden.

The lounge had a sickening smell of Febreeze that failed to mask the underlying smell of cat shit, despite Jonathan's Turkish rug having been removed to the garage, from where it would never return to domestic duty.

Emily walked over to the French windows and closed them. 'You know Theodore isn't allowed outside,' she said. 'We've only just moved in...'

'Well, he managed to get out earlier,' Jonathan said. 'It was your mum's fault.'

'My mum?' Emily said. 'How was it her fault?'

Jonathan explained that Theodore had defecated on his rug; her mother Trish had opened the window and Theodore had escaped into the garden. He had been chased by a Shih Tzu and then jet-sprayed by an angry Scot. He had taken refuge on Wally's shed roof; then rescued by Trish.

'But what's happened to his paws?' Emily said. 'They're all greasy.'

'Your mum buttered them.'

'But we don't have any butter.'

'She used the goose fat left over from Christmas... She said it would do the same job.'

Emily walked over to Theodore and picked him up.

'I think it's worked,' Jonathan said. 'He hasn't been out of my sight since your mum greased him up.'

'No wonder. What with Shih Zhus and angry Scots about,' Emily said. 'You stay home where it's safe.' She hugged him to her chest.

Theodore wriggled from her embrace, and gaining the floor again approached the French windows. He miaowed.

'You're not going anywhere,' Emily said. 'You see what you've done. Now that he's tasted freedom, he wants to be out again. Make sure he doesn't get out again. He might try to make his way back to Clementhorpe... Acomb is his home now.'

Theodore had spent most of the afternoon trying to lick the goose fat from his paws. The taste now coated his mouth. He drank lots of water but the taste would not go away. Everywhere he went the smell followed him.

As they were eating their dinner in front of the television, Jonathan commented that the lasagne had peas in it.

'My mum always does it with peas,' Emily said. 'It was the only way she could get me to eat greens when I was younger....'

'I don't think it's how the Italians do it,' Jonathan said.

They ate the lasagne while watching television. Jonathan picked the peas out of his dinner. When Emily placed her half-eaten meal on the little table by her side, Theodore had a sniff but turned his tail up at it.

Dairy spelled poison to a cat. The smell of cheese was bad enough, but then there were the garlic and onions, and to top it off – the little green balls stirred into the sauce. What sort of cat would like lasagne? wondered Theodore. Especially lasagne with peas in it.

Emily asked Jonathan, with a touch of irony, if he had managed to find time in his busy day to watch *Rear Window*. Jonathan told her that he had.

'James Stewart has a more interesting set of neighbours than we do,' Jonathan said.

Theodore's eyes widened: If only he knew.

'I can't see anything much happening around here,' Jonathan went on.

He gestured towards the back garden and the houses that backed onto theirs. 'This is just plain old York,' he said. 'Not New York.'

'Well, what do you expect? This is suburbia after all,' Emily said, picking at her food with her fork. 'You're the one who wanted to move here.'

'There was one thing that happened today that was a bit odd.'

'And what was that?'

'It's probably nothing,' Jonathan said.

Then he explained to Emily that before Theodore got out and in the ensuing commotion, the curtains in the bedroom window of the house behind had been open. Then afterwards they had been closed.

'What's so strange about that?'

'Well, there's this woman in there. Probably in her fifties or sixties. Spends all day in bed, watching television and swigging Lambrini… Looks like her daughter cares for her.'

'So?'

'I saw her looking out of the window earlier. She was scary looking. Bright red glasses and make up all over

37

her face. And she's got this little toy dog stuck in there with her.'

'How sad...'

'If I ever get like that,' Jonathan said, 'just put me out of my misery.'

Not a problem, Theodore thought, still licking his paws in front of the French windows.'

'Well, at least she's got her daughter to look after her.'

'Well, that's the thing. Before Theo got out, her bedroom curtains were open. Then there was a big commotion outside with Theo on top of the shed. And above all the noise, I heard the old woman shout: "Going to the dogs!"'

'So what? A lot of older people say stuff like that,' Emily said. 'This country's going to the dogs, you know. They're just moaning that things are different to when they were young.'

'It's the way that she said it,' Jonathan said. 'Then the curtains were closed and the window was shut... Why close the curtains in the middle of the afternoon?'

'Maybe it was all the noise outside,' Emily said. 'Her daughter probably shut the window and closed the curtains so that her mother could get some peace.'

Theodore looked at Jonathan, his brow creased, his eyes narrowed to slits.

'Could be,' Jonathan said. 'It just seems strange. And that was hours ago... They're still closed now. I hope nothing has happened to her.'

Emily walked over to the French doors and looked out at the house behind. The curtains were closed even though it was daylight.

'Oh, come on. This is Acomb. People don't just going killing people in the middle of the afternoon.'

'I'm sure you're right,' Jonathan said. 'It just seems strange.'

'She may have a headache from all the noise outside. Maybe a migraine. I get them from time to time.'

'You're probably right,' Jonathan said. 'It's probably nothing.'

They sat for some minutes, tapping at their mobile phone screens and occasionally glancing at the television screen.

After a few minutes Jonathan said, 'I think *Rear Window* is flawed.'

'How do you mean?'

'Well, the dog is killed because it's been digging in the garden. But then when Thorwald's arrested, he admits that he threw the wife's body in the East River. But the head he buried in the garden and then later packed it away in a hat box.'

'So?'

'Well, why would he bury her head separately? He would have dumped it in the river with the rest of her... Why would he treat the head differently? And why would you bury it in the focal point of the entire neighbourhood. It doesn't make sense.'

'You're thinking too much into it,' Emily said. 'You have to over-analyse things all the time. It's just a film.'

Theodore twitched back his ears and looked out of the French windows, across at the house behind. From inside the house, he heard the muffled barking of Sandy the Shih Tsu.

Emily flicked on the television. The programme comprised people being filmed while watching television programmes. The people were watching the latest James Bond film.

'It was Martini that killed my father,' a man in mustard trousers said, nodding at the screen.

'I thought it was Noilly Prat,' his wife, wearing a flowery dress, said.

Jonathan laughed at this last comment, and the end titles came on.

'I can't believe we are watching a programme about people watching television,' Emily said and sighed. 'What have we become? Next there'll be a programme about people watching people watching television.'

'I suppose it's in our nature,' Jonathan said. 'You know what they say about passing open windows.'

'We are becoming a nation of peeping toms,' Emily said, picking up her mobile phone again.

She tapped at the screen, catching up on what her friends were up to on social media.

Theodore observed the two of them, both staring at screens. He furrowed his brow. For the love of Bastet, he murmured. Peeping toms, we are nothing compared to you guys...

He could foresee the end of the human race. Their downfall would be an obsession with staring at screens. All cats had to do was wait. They would take over... one living room at a time. One day, the world would be theirs.

And people would just look on from their screens.

When Emily went upstairs to bed, Theodore followed. He settled by her side as she lay in bed reading. She soon put the book aside and stared at the ceiling.

He rubbed himself against her cheek and Emily turned on her side. She began to stroke him. Theodore stared into her green-grey eyes and purred.

But while Theodore was content with being in the moment, Emily was in a different place entirely.

The sun is shining brightly; the skies are bright blue, cloudless. There is a light breeze blowing from the sea.

Emily is standing behind a well-worn wooden bar, a glass of pina colada in front of her. She is wearing a denim skirt from Zara, t-shirt from All Saints and Kirk Geiger sandals. She takes a suck of the plastic straw and then grins at the two tanned, dark-haired men in front of her.

'But I haven't finished this one,' she says, shaking her head and laughing. 'And besides, I'm supposed to be working, aren't I?'

'This is Spain,' one of the young men says. 'Here we have an expression: *mañana.*'

'*Mañana*,' says his friend, taking a sip of beer. 'Why don't you close up now and come dancing with us? We are the only customers anyway.'

Emily laughs. 'Well, maybe a little later. I'll need to change into something different.'

Emily blinked her eyes. Theodore was staring at her, his green eyes wide, still purring.

'We are allowed to dream, you know,' she said to Theodore.

Theodore continued to stare into her face.

'I know I should be happy with all this,' Emily said. 'I have a house, a job, a boyfriend. And you of course… I should be happy.'

Theodore agreed.

Cats didn't have much choice when it came to houses or even owners. They made the most of what they had and got on with it. Dreaming of what life may have been like if another human had taken them in or if they lived in that house and not this house was completely futile. You just got on with what you had.

When Emily turned off her bedside light, Theodore snuggled into her side but found he couldn't sleep.

He jumped down from the bed, crossed the landing and went into one of the back bedrooms. He jumped up onto the windowsill.

The kitchen light was on in Ellen's house. The light in Tessa's bedroom was also on, lighting up the sunflowers on the curtains.

He watched as Ellen appeared in the kitchen. She had her arms under her mother's shoulders, as she dragged her body across the kitchen floor. Tessa was without her wig. Tufts of grey white hair stuck out from her scalp.

Ellen lay her mother down on the linoleum. Then she removed her necklace, ear rings and wedding ring. She placed the items in a little wicker basket on the kitchen side.

She opened the back door and then pulled her mother out into the night. She pulled her across the overgrown lawn, her mother's two feet making two long furrows, two feet part, across the lawn.

They stopped in front of the shed. Ellen went inside and began making room. Five minutes later, she shut the shed door and returned inside the house. A minute later the light went off in her mother's room and the light went on in the next window.

Theodore watched as Ellen approached her bedroom window and looked outside into the night. She was wearing a grey t-shirt that was too small for her, her chest pressing against the soft cotton. Her brown wavy hair was tied back. She looked across at Theodore and smiled. Then she drew her curtains.

Theodore looked across at the pink and blue curtains. He made out princesses riding unicorns.

And then the window went black as Ellen turned off the light.

Suburban Psycho

The sunflower curtains in Tessa Black's bedroom remained closed all the next day. From the back bedroom window Theodore observed the house. Midmorning, he spied Ellen in the kitchen making herself a mug of tea. She was dressed in baggy grey jogging bottoms and a blue shirt that had belonged to her father, three buttons undone.

At lunchtime she heated soup on the hob and poured it into a bowl. She carried it along with half a loaf of bread into the dining room and ate bent over the dining table.

Theodore noted several large brown envelopes on the table, an iPad, as well as a large album with a black shiny cover.

He heard Sandy yapping but there was no sign of the Shih Tzu. She must be locked in the bedroom, thought Theodore, licking his paws; the taste of goose fat still strong on his tongue.

He watched as the blind man next door to Ellen let his guide dog Lucy out in the garden for her fifteen minutes of freedom. Later he watched as the man located Lucy's morning turd, by sense of smell he presumed, and popped it in a little black bag which he popped into his black wheelie bin.

Downstairs Jonathan was watching *Psycho*, another Hitchcock film. Theodore settled down on the cushion beside him; he preferred black and white films to colour ones, like most cats.

'It's strange,' Jonathan said, 'but the curtains of the house behind haven't been opened today.'

I know, purred Theodore in agreement, rubbing against Jonathan's side.

'I wonder if she has done something to her,' Jonathan went on, rubbing Theodore behind the ears. 'The dog hasn't been let out today either. It's been yapping all morning.'

Theodore purred in agreement. Dogs should learn to keep quiet. Yapping and barking all the time... Disturbing the peace. There ought to be a law against it. Then they settled back and watched *Psycho*.

About halfway through the film, a man wearing a black beanie and carrying a yellow bucket appeared in front of the French windows. Jonathan's reaction was to take hold of one of his metal walking sticks and wave it at the intruder.

'I'm here to clean the windows,' the man shouted through the glass. He waved a window cleaning blade in the air.

Jonathan managed to get to his feet with his crutches and hobble over to the French windows being careful not to put any weight on his booted foot.

He opened the doors and said, 'I didn't think we had a window cleaner. We've only just moved in...'

There was a blur of grey by his feet and then he watched as Theodore raced across the lawn and disappeared into the hedge at the back of the garden.

'The cat,' Jonathan said, 'he's not supposed to go outside.'

'Well, it's out now,' the window cleaner said. 'I'm Norman. I had a call this morning,' he went on. 'A lady... She said the windows needed cleaning as a matter of urgency, and I was to come straight round.

She told me to let myself in through the side gate and that you'd be sitting on the sofa watching telly.'

Trish, thought Jonathan. She must have phoned a window cleaner.

'Don't you have a colour telly?' Norman said, looking at the frozen picture on the television screen.

'The film is in black and white,' Jonathan said.

'I didn't think they made them in black and white anymore.'

'It's an old film. *Psycho*.'

'Never heard of it,' Norman said. 'Well, I don't have time to be sitting watching telly when there's windows to clean... Do you want me to do inside as well as outside?'

'How much does it cost for both?'

'Twice as much. It's twice the work, isn't it?'

'I think both,' Jonathan said. 'I don't know when they were last cleaned, but they do look a bit grimy. Inside and out.'

'It'll be twenty quid.'

Jonathan nodded, hoping that he had twenty pounds in his wallet.'

'I used to clean the windows of that house over there,' Norman said, nodding at the house behind. 'But then they stopped. After what happened... Terrible business that.'

'What happened?' Jonathan said.

'Terrible business,' Norman said. 'I'd better be getting on.'

He then went into the kitchen to fill his bucket up.

Stuart was in his garden, clipping his hedge though it did not look like it needed clipping.

Theodore watched him from the top of Wally's shed. He looked at the next garden and the shed in the corner. A grey hand jutted out from below the bottom of the door.

Ellen opened the kitchen door and lit a cigarette. She looked over at Theodore and then turned and followed his gaze. She spotted the hand sticking out from the bottom of the shed door and began to cross the garden towards it.

'Got a spare ciggie?' Stuart shouted over the hedge at her.

Ellen stopped and turned to face her neighbour. She was standing directly between Stuart and the shed. She walked towards Stuart taking her cigarettes from her shirt pocket as she went.

'You ever going to buy any?'

'I've got some baccie but it's not the same.'

He took the cigarette. 'You got a light?'

Ellen passed her lighter over the hedge, and Theodore noticed Stuart glancing at her chest that pushed against her shirt.

'So, how's Tessa today?' Stuart asked and took a drag on his cigarette.

Ellen glanced up at Theodore. 'Same as ever,' she said.

'I don't know how you do it,' Stuart said. 'You must have the patience of a saint putting up with her.'

Ellen looked at her neighbour. 'Someone has to do it, haven't they?'

'Aye. I suppose so. Well, I'd better get back it.'

Theodore watched as Stuart finished his cigarette, took one last appreciative glance at Ellen's chest; then went back inside his shed.

Ellen walked over to the small shed in the corner of her garden. She opened the door.

Her mother fell out onto the lawn.

'Let's get you back inside,' Ellen said. 'We can't have you waving at people, can we now?'

She picked her mother up and pushed her as far back as she would go. She then shut the shed door and inspected it to make sure nothing was on display.

'That'll have to do,' she said to herself. 'For now…'

Before she went back inside, she glanced up at Theodore.

'Thanks for letting me know,' she murmured over at him.

Theodore closed his eyes, believing that that would make him invisible.

He opened them again when he heard footsteps approaching.

'I've brought you a mug of tea,' Marjorie said. 'And a slice of quiche.'

'What type of quiche is it today, Madge?' Wally said from inside the shed.

'Bork,' Marjorie said.

'Ah! Beef and pork,' Wally said. 'That's my favourite.'

'I put a bit of crackling in it too.'

'You shouldn't have,' Wally said. 'You'll be fattening me up…' He laughed.

'Get away with you,' Marjorie said. 'There's not an ounce of fat on you!'

'Theo!' Jonathan called.

Theodore turned.

Jonathan was standing in front of the French windows.

'The window cleaner's gone now,' he said. 'You can come back inside.'

Theodore blinked no; he was staying where he was.

Jonathan began to make his way towards him, using his crutches trying not to put any weight on his broken foot. He reached the corner of the garden when his neighbour's head appeared above the hedge.

'That cat of yours has taken up residence on my shed roof,' Wally said.

Jonathan looked up and saw Theodore looking down.

'That's Theo,' Jonathan said. 'He came with the girlfriend. He shouldn't be out of the house.'

'That's what I told her,' Wally said. 'But I don't mind if he wants to sit up there. You see, we are allies of sorts.'

'Allies? Oh, you mean the Scot?'

'Aye, Stuart.'

Wally told Jonathan that Stuart was married to Leslie, who worked in a bank in the centre of York. They had two children, Dougie and Daisy, and Stuart was a stay-at-home dad. When the children were at school Stuart spent the time in his shed. When they weren't at school he spent most of the time in his shed.

'No idea what he gets up to in there,' Wally said. 'But he spends a lot of time in that shed of his. All you can hear is tap-tap-tapping and then a lot of cursing.'

'I wonder what he's up to in there.'

'Beats me... Have you met your other neighbours?'

Jonathan shook his head.

'Well, on your other side you have Steve and Sam. They have a little Chihuahua. Fattest little dog I ever saw.'

'I'll keep an eye out,' Jonathan said.

'Then there's Geoffrey in the bungalow over there. He was a pilot but lost his sight. Spent too long staring into the sun...'

Wally laughed and Jonathan wondered if he was joking.

'What about my neighbours behind?' Jonathan said.

'The Blacks?' Wally said. 'It's just Ellen and her mum Tessa now... Colin died some years ago. Very sudden it was. He was here one day… Then one day he was gone. Whoosh! Just like that.'

Jonathan wondered a moment at the 'Whoosh'.

'Tessa hasn't been well of late,' Wally went on. 'She has good days and bad days. Mainly bad days… She used to take her dog Sandy to West Bank Park every day. I saw her one day. It was after her husband had gone. She had a bottle in one hand and she was pulling hair from her head with the other. One hair at a time. Carried on doing that till she had no hair left. That's why she wears a wig. Pulled all her hair out.

'She never got over him. Fell apart she did… Never leaves the house these days. I don't think she even gets out of bed some days.'

'What about her daughter?'

'I suppose Ellen does the best she can. She'll be on that carer's allowance. She's never had a job. Stays at home and looks after her mum. That's not much of a life for a young girl. In your twenties you should be out and about. Gallivanting…'

Wally took a drink of tea.

'There's another daughter,' Wally said, remembering. 'Penny. Aye, Penny… Colin was a keen stamp collector…'

Jonathan looked puzzled.

'Penny Black! Like the stamp,' Wally said grinning.

'I see,' Jonathan said.

'Penny visits now and then but she moved away. Lives somewhere down south I believe. Went off to university and didn't come back. Hardly ever visits.'

'That's a pity,' Jonathan said.

'Bad it is,' Wally said, 'Ellen being left to look after her mum like that.'

'You didn't hear Tessa shouting the other day, did you? You know when Stuart was trying to jet wash our cat…'

'Can't say I did,' Wally said. 'There was all the commotion out here, and my hearing's not what it was.'

'I was just a little worried about her. I heard her shouting. Then when I looked up again the curtains were closed and the window shut.'

Walter looked across. 'She'll just be having a lie in... Watching TV in bed. Like I said, some days she doesn't even get up.'

'I'm sure you're right,' Jonathan said uncertainly, glancing up at the window with the sunflower curtains.

When Emily got home from work, Jonathan told her about the curtains not having been opened in Tessa's bedroom all day and the dog yapping from inside the house.

He had a can of beer in one hand and took a swig. 'I think something might have happened to her. I really do.'

'Are you serious?' Emily said, hands on hips. 'She's probably got a migraine and closed the curtains. And the dog was barking so her daughter shut it in another room so it wouldn't disturb her.'

'I'm not so sure.'

'Oh please,' Emily said. 'I've had a long day at work. This isn't what I need when I get home.'

She crossed to the table and picked up a packet of painkillers. 'I'm sure you shouldn't be drinking when you're on these. You're imagining things.'

'I was just telling you what happened today,' Jonathan said. 'I'm just a bit concerned about her.'

'Where is Theo?' Emily asked.

'He got out again,' Jonathan said. 'A window cleaner came and I opened the doors... He was on Wally's shed roof earlier.'

Emily crossed to the glass doors. She opened them wide and called his name. A moment later Theodore appeared from the back hedge and trotted across the lawn. Emily scooped him up and hugged him to her.

'The window cleaner mentioned something happening with the house behind, and then Wally said that the father had died suddenly. Maybe the daughter, Ellen she's called, killed him too. She might be working her way through the whole family...'

'Give it a rest,' Emily said. She put Theodore down and closed the French windows. 'I'm going to have a shower, and when I come back I don't want to hear any more about it.'

She marched out of the lounge and into the hallway.

'Just be careful of the shower rail,' Jonathan called after her. 'It's loose and needs fixing.'

But Emily was already in the downstairs shower room, the door pushed closed behind her but left ajar. A few moments later Theodore heard water. He approached the door and then noticed a white rectangle of card lying on the floor by the front door.

It was a business card from Norman, the window cleaner. He must have posted it through the front door after he left.

On the card was written:

N. BATES

PROFFESIONAL WINDOW CLEANING SERVICES

NO SMEAR GARANTIE

Theodore stared a moment at the slip of paper. Then his attention was drawn by a buzzing overhead. It was a bee.

Theodore swiped at it as it flew past him. He turned round and chased after the bee. As the bee rose in the air, Theodore launched himself, a paw held out at the intruding insect. He just missed it. He turned again and saw the bee fly into the shower room. Theodore followed, pushing open the door so that he could fit through.

'Is there somebody there?' Emily said, over the spray of the water from the shower.

The shower room was tiled in shiny white and had a white shower curtain dividing it into two. From behind the curtain, Theodore made out Emily's outline, her silhouette cast onto the plastic curtain by the window behind her.

The bee buzzed within the confined space of the shower room, unable to navigate a way out. Theodore crouched in the doorway waiting his chance.

'Is that you Jonathan?' Emily said from behind the shower curtain.

When the bee buzzed past the shower curtain the third time, Theodore chose his moment. His paws outstretched, he launched himself into the air. He saw the bee pass just in front of his paws as he dived forwards. Then his claws snagged on the shower curtain, ripping the thin plastic sheet.

Emily screamed, as the shower curtain and metal rail came down on top of her.

Not again, thought Theodore, as the shower head spun round, sending out a spray of water at him. Another soaking.

Emily stood naked and screamed again, but this time it was Theodore's name that came from her lips.

The Writing on the Doors

'No Perambulation. In Front Street, Acomb, still much of the village character. The most notable house is Acomb House, mostly mid-Georgian, with a two-storeyed mid-projection. The top storey is later."
Sir Nikolaus Pevsner, *The Buildings of England Yorkshire: York & The East Riding*

Most people think of Acomb as a big suburb of York, inhabited by plumbers and decorators, and retired plumbers and decorators, and they wouldn't be far wrong.

But it was once a village on the outskirts of the city, and part of the West Riding of Yorkshire. Its name came from the Old English for oak tree. It was only in 1937 that Acomb was swallowed up by the City of York and transformed into a suburb of the city.

The twentieth century saw the population of Acomb rise dramatically with housing built on the farmland and by the twenty first century Acomb had a population of twenty thousand people.

Jonathan was sitting on the sofa, reading the Pevsner guide he had picked up in Fossgate Books some years before. He glanced at the brief entry for Acomb. 'No perambulation,' he read aloud. 'He didn't even bother getting out of his car... Probably just said to his wife from the back seat, "Keep driving!"'

Theodore flicked back his good ear. Writing about architecture was the equivalent of miaowing about cat biscuits in his opinion. And besides, Pevsner might have had the right idea by not getting out of his car, he thought, thinking of some of his new neighbours. He looked out of the French windows at the houses behind and then jumped down to the floor.

Theodore paced in front of the glass doors. A woman had been killed and all Jonathan could do was to read architectural criticism.

Theodore knew that Ellen had killed her mother; Jonathan only suspected as much; Emily didn't believe a word of it. It was going to be down to him to expose Ellen.

He thought of the crime dramas he had watched on television with Emily in the pre-Jonathan days. The 'whodunnits'. Theodore knew who had done it: Ellen.

Then he thought of the *Columbos* he had seen, where the viewer knew who had done it but watched to see how Columbo would prove how they had done it. The 'howdunnits'.

But this was not a howdunnit. Theodore licked his paws in contemplation. This was not a whodunit or a howdunnit, but a *how-do-I-prove-to-the-humans-that-she-did-it?*

He paced in front of the sofa, where Jonathan sat reading his book. He wagged his tail from side to side. He went into the kitchen. His litter box was still in the corner. The wrong type of litter, he remembered.

He headed towards the litter box. He urinated in the corner and then patted the clay pellets with his front paws until they turned to sludge. It really was the wrong type of litter. He emerged a minute later, his paws coated with urine-soaked clay.

Back in the lounge Jonathan was still reading his architectural guide to York. Theodore approached the French windows again. If Jonathan had any doubts that a murder had been committed he was going to have to spell it out to him.

He began on the right hand door and worked his way to the left. As everyone knows, cats both read and write from right to left. When he had finished he stood back to inspect his paw-writing.

'She killed her mother,' it was supposed to say.

Instead it looked like a lot of muddy smears across the glass. Theodore blinked. This writing business was trickier than he had presumed. He glanced at Jonathan on the sofa. His head was tilted back and his eyes were closed. He hadn't even noticed Theodore's attempts at writing.

Theodore settled down on the other sofa. He was going to have to think long and hard about the situation, he realised. It was definitely a three-nap problem; he would need at least fifty minutes to consider the problem.

He crossed his forelegs in front of him, placed his head in the V between his legs and closed his eyes, readying himself to enter into deep analytical thought, worthy of a detective of his status.

Before his fifty minutes had elapsed, there was a tapping at the front door and then he heard a key in the lock and the front door opened.

'Jonathan?' Trish called out, before entering the lounge. 'Are you in here?'

'I haven't run off,' Jonathan said from the sofa, not bothering to turn round.

'I've brought you some lunch,' Trish said. 'Soup and a sandwich.'

'Sounds good,' Jonathan said from the sofa.

'Did the window cleaner come the other day?' Trish asked, staring over Jonathan's head at the French windows.

'Yes,' Jonathan said, 'he did both inside and out.'

'Did he now?' Trish said.

She crossed to the glass doors and waved a finger across the muddy smears. She held her forefinger in front of her face. 'They're still dirty. On the inside.'

'He did the insides,' Jonathan said. 'I was here when he did them.'

'Well, he didn't do a very good job,' Trish said. 'These window cleaners... They're a law unto themselves.'

Jonathan pointed past Trish at the house behind. 'I think something might have happened to the woman behind. I haven't seen her since the other morning. Her curtains haven't been opened. And the dog has been yapping all the time. I think it's been locked in a room.'

'Why Jonathan,' Trish said, 'are you developing an imagination?'

Trish had evidently not forgotten Christmas Day. They had all been watching *The Hobbit: The Desolation of Smaug*, in which a party of dwarves and their hobbit ally continue their quest to reclaim their kingdom, journeying through the forest of their ancestral enemy, the elves, and finally face the dragon Smaug that had driven the dwarves from their home, when Jonathan woke from a post-prandial nap and said: 'Well, this is all a bit far-fetched.'

'You'll be reading Terry Pratchett next,' Trish added.

'I think the daughter Ellen snapped and smothered her with a pillow,' Jonathan said. 'I heard her mother say, "It's going to the dogs". I think she meant her daughter's inheritance. She was going to leave everything to the RSPCA...'

'You're reading too much into it... This is Suburbia. People don't commit murder in the suburbs. You want to move to a village if you want that sort of thing. We have homicides, patricides, matricides, suicides... Even the odd felinicide,' she said, casting a sideways glance at Theodore.

Theodore folded back his ears and looked at a patch of floor. He was glad he didn't live in a village.

'Well, I'd better put the soup on.' Trish said. 'I don't have all day.'

Jonathan was relieved that the soup was tomato and the sandwich cheese. He ate off a tray on his lap and watched the news on television while Trish cleaned the kitchen.

After he had finished his lunch and Trish had washed up the dishes, she announced that she was going back to Acaster Mildew, a village just outside of York, its existence known only by those that actually live there, and the postman, of course.

'I don't like to leave Pat too long,' Trish said, referring to her husband and Emily's father.

When they had met, they both went by Pat. But as everyone knows, you cannot have two Pats in a house, so rather than her husband becoming Trick she had offered to be Trish, and that was the name she now went by, though deep down she was and would always be a Pat.

'You know he's always having those little accidents,' Trish went on. 'We wouldn't want him bleeding to death in his workshop while I'm out, would we now?'

'No, certainly not,' Jonathan said nodding.

And with that, Trish turned and left.

Norman, the window cleaner, returned later that afternoon. Theodore watched from the front window as a white van with N Bates Window Cleaner pulled up outside the house and Norman jumped out. He went straight round the side of the house and let himself in through the gate.

Jonathan managed to get to his feet and opened the French windows to let the window cleaner in.

'Didn't you clean the windows only the other day?'

Norman explained that he had been called by Trish. 'She said there were some smears. She wasn't very happy about it. I thought I'd better see for myself. I told her when I left yesterday, they were sparkling clean, but she insisted that they were covered in smears. On the inside.'

'I hadn't noticed any smears,' Jonathan said.

'The lady said there were smears. Gave me a right earful.'

Norman bent down and began to examine the glass. 'Looks like muddy paw prints.'

He pushed his forefinger through the muddy streaks and then raised it in front of his nose. 'It's like clay.'

'It's probably...' Jonathan said and then stopped himself as Norman dabbed his forefinger on his tongue. 'It's like clay.'

Theodore looked on from the doorway as Norman took a cloth and wiped the glass clean.

'There's nothing to pay this time,' Norman said once he was done and satisfied that there were no more smears.

'Are you sure?'

'Yes,' Norman said. 'No smear guarantee and all that... Besides I had finished for the day. I don't have that many customers at the moment...'

'Maybe it's down to the name,' Jonathan said. 'You know Norman Bates...'

'What's up with my name? Norman was my dad's name, and his dad's before that. It's a good name.'

'Norman Bates was the one who slashed the girl in the shower. You know in *Pyscho*?'

Norman shook his head. 'Don't know about him.'

'He dressed up as his dead mother. You must know it. It's the film I had on yesterday.'

'Don't know anything about slashing a girl in the shower,' he said, still shaking his head. 'Or dressing up as a dead mother...'

'It was in the film,' Jonathan explained. 'It was a Hitchcock film. *Psycho*... You must have heard of it. 'He's the serial killer in *Psycho*. Anthony Perkins played Norman Bates.'

'I've never heard of this Perkins,' Norman said. 'It was him who slashed this girl?'

'The actor who played Norman Bates slashed the girl. You must know it. It was a big film. They remade it. He kills this girl in the shower.'

'*Psycho*? No, never heard of it. And Norman Bates is this psycho in the film, right?'

'Yes. Maybe that's what's putting people off calling you. They see your name and think twice.'

'It explains a lot,' Norman said. 'But I've had all these leaflets and business cards printed up. They cost me twenty quid for two hundred at the service station.'

Norman took a business card from his back pocket and handed it to Jonathan.

Jonathan took the card. 'It says N. Bates,' Jonathan said, handing the card back to Norman. 'You could always change your first name to another name that begins with N.'

'Like what?'

'What about Nigel?'

'Nigel? I'm not sure about that. My family have always been Normans.'

'Nigel Bates wouldn't scare customers away like Norman does. You don't get many mass murderers called Nigel.'

Theodore's eyes widened. I think you might be forgetting Nigel 'Cat Killer' Hibbs.

Nigel Hibbs murdered up to 70 cats in the village of Newbold Verdon, Leicestershire, by placing sodium cyanide-laced sardines in his back garden in a killing spree that lasted two years. When arrested, the police found enough poison under his bed to kill 1,500 cats as well as an empty sardine tin, latex gloves, face masks and newspaper cuttings about the disappearances.

'Nigel?' Norman said. 'I suppose it sounds all right. Nigel Bates.'

'So, are you going to be Nigel from now on?'

'Yes, I think I might give it a go. Just for business like.'

While Jonathan and Nigel were discussing the changing of names, Theodore slipped through the French windows that had been left open and trotted across the lawn to the back of the garden.

Geoffrey Offers to Help

He watched from the bottom of the hedge as Ellen dragged her mother out of the shed by her feet and laid her out on the unkempt lawn.

She then pulled the green wheelie bin next to the corpse and swung open its lid. She bent down and picked up her mother in a fireman's lift. Then she dropped her into the wheelie bin, head first.

Rigor mortis had set in, and her mother's feet stood proud of the top of the bin. Ellen pulled the lid down on the legs but the bin lid refused to close. She tried to push the legs further down into the bin but they still jutted out at odd angles, so that she couldn't close the bin lid without a foot sticking out.

She pushed the bin on its side and went inside the shed. She emerged a minute later with a rusty old axe.

She pulled her mother out by her feet until her knees were exposed and then began to hack at her shins.

Theodore heard an excited bark and then watched as Lucy led Geoffrey to the hedge that formed the boundary between his house and the Blacks.

Geoffrey stood beside the hedge and heard Ellen chopping at her mother's legs. 'Doing a spot of gardening?' he said. 'A spring tidy, is it?'

Ellen paused from her efforts. She stood up and faced her neighbour, who was wearing his mirrored sunglasses and a shirt that had been buttoned up wrong so that one collar was higher than the other.

'Just trying to get this old tree in the wheelie bin,' she said. 'Can't seem to get it all in…'

'I've got a chipper in the garage,' Geoffrey said. 'You could use that... Haven't used it in years what with my eyesight going but I'm sure we could get it going. You'd have to give me a hand looking for it... If we put it through the chipper, you won't have any problem fitting it all in your wheelie bin.'

'A chipper?' Ellen said. 'I don't think a chipper is really necessary... It's just these big branches I need to fit in.'

'Well, the offer's there,' Geoffrey said.

Lucy had her face pushed into the hedge. She whined excitedly; the dog could see the dead woman on the other side. She clawed at the ground in front of the hedge and barked.

'Lucy!' Geoffrey admonished. 'Whatever's got into you?' He yanked on her lead.

Lucy barked again.

'That's quite enough,' Geoffrey said, pulling on her harness. 'She wants her walk,' he said to Ellen. 'I'd better get her to the park. We're normally in West Bank by now.'

'You get off,' Ellen said. 'I'll soon sort this out; don't you worry about us.'

'Well, give my regards to your mother,' Geoffrey said. 'Haven't seen her for a while.'

'No,' Ellen said. 'She doesn't get out that much these days.'

'Oh, she should. A bit of fresh air would do her the world of good.'

'I think it might be a bit late for that,' Ellen said under her breath.

Geoffrey shrugged and pulled his dog away, Lucy still barking.

'I really don't know what's got into her,' he said, pulling Lucy across the lawn, back towards the bungalow.

Theodore watched from the bottom of the hedge as Ellen finished hacking through her mother's legs, threw the dismembered body parts into the wheelie bin and closed the lid. She then went back into the shed and came out with a spade. She wedged the spade down the inside of the wheelie bin and closed the lid once more.

Well at least he was not the only one to know the truth, Theodore thought. Lucy had also seen the dead woman. He wasn't the sole witness anymore. But why did it have to be a dog? A dog detective on the case! Whatever next?

Then he heard Marjorie shouting for her husband, louder as she drew closer to the shed. She was almost at the shed door before Wally opened it.

Theodore turned and looked back at his own house. Through the French windows he saw Jonathan sitting on the sofa, his booted foot propped up on the coffee table.

Wally, Jonathan and Geoffrey...

Deaf, dumb and blind...

He was definitely up against it.

He closed his eyes, deep in thought, and only opened them when he heard Emily call his name. She was standing in front of the French windows. Theodore chose to ignore her; he stayed where he was.

He looked across at the green wheelie bin that stood by Ellen's shed. Emily soon gave up and went back inside. Theodore waited.

In the kitchen Ellen was staring out of the window. Her eyes were red rimmed from crying. She took a gulp from a wine glass. She spotted Theodore in the bottom of the back hedge and caught his eye. She smiled at him.

From behind, Theodore heard Emily almost shout, 'I told you not to let him out. And what do you do? Let him out... Three days in a row.'

63

Theodore looked again from Ellen to the wheelie bin and waited.

Night-time came. Ellen went out the back door. She pulled the wheelie bin down the side of the house. Theodore waited for her to disappear before emerging from the bottom of the hedge and setting off after her. He followed behind her, along Constantine Crescent and out onto York Road. She didn't look back.

There were few people in the street and the people they passed took little notice of the young woman with a wheelie bin and the large grey cat that trailed twenty yards behind.

Eventually Ellen turned left and entered through the gate that led into the grounds of St Stephen's church.

Theodore paused at the gate, and as Ellen passed between two great elms, Theodore began to trot after her.

He passed to the east of the church, under the curtilage of a gigantic beech tree. Before him there was a cemetery, stretching down the hill. Gravestones stood high, low, or lay flat on the ground. There were plenty of places for a cat to hide.

Near the bottom of the hillside, Ellen had stopped. The headstones in this part of the cemetery were of hard black granite and not the softer sandstones and limestones of the ones further up the hill.

She pulled the wheelie bin to the side of a grave. She pulled out the spade and began to remove the turf from the grave and put it to one side.

Once the turf was removed, she began to shovel the sandy soil to the other side. Within half an hour she had dug a hole three feet deep.

Theodore approached cautiously, careful not to make any sound. He crouched behind a headstone. He watched as Ellen pulled her mother from the wheelie bin and laid her in the newly opened grave. She placed the bottoms of her legs at the foot of the hole.

She stood for a moment over the grave.

Theodore studied the headstone. It was inscribed in gold letters on the black background:

'Colin Black
1954 – 2007

Beloved husband and father,
A light that burned bright, snuffed out too soon

R.I.P

Theodore watched as Ellen wiped tears from her eyes. Then she began to backfill the hole.

Verge Wars

On arriving home from work, Steve always parked his Audi on the grass verge in front of Linda's house. He couldn't park in front of his own house, as there was a lime tree growing there and all the other spaces along the side of the road had been taken.

What had once been a little rectangle of green in front of Linda's house had been reduced to churned-up dried mud. Linda was determined to change that.

After Steve had set off to work that Friday morning, she scurried out of her house, a trowel in one hand and a large bag in the other. She then proceeded to plant daffodils in the verge in front of her house. Linda wasn't one to complain to the council; she was a believer in direct action.

Theodore watched from the front window as his purple clad neighbour squatted down and planted the yellow flowers.

Later a coach of Chinese tourists drove by, very slowly, and Theodore felt a hundred small handheld devices point at him from behind the coach windows, a hundred small screens that now held his image.

He realised he was part of the picture, a part of the suburban scene: the cat in the window of the semi-detached house.

Curtains for Sandy

Sandy the Shih Zhu was twelve years old. She had been utterly devoted to her owner Tessa. When Tessa had taken to her bed after her husband Colin died, Sandy had stuck it out with her.

He had watched her drink bottle after bottle of Lambrini or Pinot Grigio from her basket in the corner of the room. He had kept her company while she watched depressing daytime television. He had witnessed her wee the bed on numerous occasions.

Now the bedroom door was closed and her owner was dead. It was two days since she had been fed. She scratted at the brown carpet in front of the bedroom door. She whined. She yapped. She weed in the corner. She yapped some more. She scratted at the carpet some more. She weed in the corner once more. Finally she heard footsteps approach. Sandy yapped with excitement. Finally she would be released.

The bedroom door swung open.

'If you don't shut up,' Ellen said, entering the bedroom. 'You're going to get it.'

Sandy yapped some more.

'I've warned you,' she said and shut the bedroom door behind her.

'Is that dog ever going to be quiet?' Jonathan asked Theodore. They were sitting on the sofa, watching *North by Northwest*.

On the screen, Eva Marie Saint is hanging by her fingers to the rocky face of Mount Rushmore. 'What happened to your first two marriages?' she asks Cary Grant, who is playing advertising executive Robert O Thornhill, mistaken for a government agent by a group of foreign spies and chased across the country.

'My wives divorced me,' he replies.

'Why?' asks Eva Marie Saint, who is playing the part of gorgeous blonde Eve Kendall.

'They said I led too dull a life,' Cary Grant says.

Yap, yap, went Sandy from the house behind.

Jonathan paused the film.

'I really can't concentrate on this,' Jonathan said to Theodore. 'What with that racket coming from behind...'

They both looked over at the window with drawn curtains.

Theodore heard Sandy's yaps take a different, more desperate tone. He watched as Sandy's head suddenly appeared in the window, the flowery curtains parting for a moment, before coming together again, as the dog dropped out of sight.

'Did you see that?' Jonathan said.

Theodore blinked yes and sat up.

A few seconds later, Sandy's head appeared once more in the bottom of the window.

Both Jonathan and Theodore watched the window opposite, as the flowery curtains were repeatedly parted and the little dog's head appeared again. The curtains remained slightly apart, and the dog managed to scrabble up onto the window sill, only to fall back down again.

'It must be locked in the bedroom,' Jonathan said.

Theodore agreed with another blink of his eyes.

Then the yapping turned to a whimper.

Then a yelping.

Then nothing.

'Do you think something might have happened to the dog now?' Jonathan asked.

Theodore jumped down from the sofa and approached the French windows. He miaowed affirmatively.

Jonathan took his crutches and got to his feet. Careful not to put any pressure on his booted broken foot, he crossed to the French windows and joined Theodore.

The curtains were closed.

'I think something has happened to that dog,' he said.

I think that was curtains for Sandy, agreed Theodore.

'Ted Bundy started on animals and worked his way up to humans,' Jonathan said. 'Let's hope she's not working her way down the chain... Cats could be next.'

Theodore pondered his words. Working her way down the chain? I think you might have that tail about whiskers...

Jonathan opened the right hand window absent-mindedly and looked across at the house behind. It was now deathly quiet.

He didn't notice Theodore slipping through the open window until it was too late.

'Not again,' he said to himself.

The Beginning of the End of the Roman Empire

"But we read that Severus had his palace in this City, and here at the houre of death gave up his last breath with these words, I entred upon a state everywhere troublesome, and I leave it peaceable even to the Britains. *His bodie was carried forth here to the funerall fire by the soldiors, after the military fashion, and committed to the flames, honoured with Justs and Turneaments of his soldiours and his owne sonnes, in a place beneath this City Westward nere to Ackham where is to bee seene a great mount of earth raised up, which, as Raulph Niger hath recorded, was in his time of Severus called Sivers."*
William Camden

And so, in Ackham (now spelled Acomb), York; on a hillside to the west of the city, while his sons and soldiers played games, Septimus Severus' body was turned to cinders; signifying the beginning of the end of the Roman Empire.

Over 1,800 years later, near this very spot, a cinder caught in Ellen's eye. She blinked furiously and wiped at it; then swore.

She was standing over a hole she had dug in the flower bed. She stuck the spade in the lawn and stared over at the corner of the hedge, over which grey smoke billowed. She walked over.

'That smoke is coming right at me,' she shouted across at Wally, who was standing over the garden fire, a stick in his hand, a red cap on his head.

Wally turned and grinned at Ellen. 'I can't change the direction of the wind. But you could always try standing somewhere else.'

'You're always burning stuff,' Ellen said.

'There's a lot of garden waste this time of year.'

'You could always use your wheelie bin like everyone else.'

'I'd never fit it all in,' Wally said. 'They're too small.'

Elle thought back to the difficulty of getting her mother into the bin. She agreed with Wally that they were a bit small. 'You might have a point there,' she said.

'If you want to chuck anything on, go ahead.'

Ellen glanced back at the shed, in which Sandy waited to be buried. 'I think I can manage,' she said.

'Well, if you change your mind, just chuck it over over the hedge.'

'I'd better get on,' Ellen said.

She crossed the garden to the shed and retrieved the Shih Zhu. She carried it across the lawn by its paws as if it were a handbag coated in faux fur.

Theodore watched from the bottom of the hedge as Ellen deposited the dog into the hole in the garden and began to shovel soil over the top.

He turned, exited the hedge and raced back across the lawn. He saw Jonathan sitting on the sofa and Jonathan saw him. Theodore noticed a look of alarm on Jonathan's face.

He carried on running, towards him, forgetting that there was glass in the French windows that separated them; glass that had been so thoroughly cleaned by Nigel, it was invisible to the eye.

When he opened his eyes again, he was lying on the patio. Jonathan was standing over him, balanced on his crutches. He wasn't sure how long he had been knocked out. He invoked Bastet to bring about a curse upon window cleaners before getting to his paws.

Then he remembered the dead dog.

He began to make his way on wobbly legs back towards the lawn.

'Are you OK?' said Jonathan, following. 'Are you sure you don't need a lie down or something?'

But Theodore kept going, back across the lawn, weaving his way towards the hedge.

And Jonathan followed after him.

A Spot of Gardening

Jonathan saw Ellen over the hedge, digging in her garden. Theodore had disappeared into the bottom of the hedge. Jonathan approached, trying not to put any weight on his broken foot.

When Jonathan reached the hedge, Ellen was compacting the soil with the back of a spade.

She had her back to him and Jonathan surveyed her rear, clad in tight blue jogging pants, before asking, 'Have you seen my cat?'

Ellen turned, surprised, holding the spade as you would a weapon. She stared at Jonathan. 'What?' she said.

'My cat,' Jonathan said. 'He got out. I saw him going into the hedge. I thought he must have got through.'

'I haven't seen a cat,' Ellen said.

'Doing a spot of gardening?' Jonathan asked.

Ellen stuck the spade into the ground 'What does it look like?'

'I don't know,' Jonathan said. 'I suppose you could be burying something...'

Ellen took a step towards him. 'Burying something? Like what?'

Jonathan thought 'dog' but instead said 'treasure'.

'Treasure?' Ellen said, shaking her head. 'Why would I be burying treasure in the garden?'

'You know,' Jonathan said, thinking what to say next so that she wouldn't think him stupid. 'It's Easter soon. You might be planning an Easter Egg hunt...'

She shook her head and folded her arms across her chest. 'I am not planning an Easter egg hunt. I'm just doing a spot of gardening.'

Jonathan looked across at the patch where she had been digging. The soil had been turned over in just one place. The rest of the flower bed was still overgrown. The surface covered by dense weeds. He noticed that the lawn hadn't been cut for a long time. He noted the little dog turds scattered about. 'A spot of gardening?' he said.

'Yes, a spot of gardening.'

'Yes, of course... Nice weather for it.'

'Is that all?'

'I haven't heard your dog today...'

'No,' Ellen said. 'Sandy is sleeping. Must have tired herself out.'

'Right,' said Jonathan, looking up at the bedroom window. 'Upstairs.'

'Yes, upstairs,' Ellen said. 'She sleeps on my mum's bed.'

'They're both sleeping?'

'Yes. They're both sleeping upstairs.'

'The curtains...' Jonathan said, 'they haven't been opened in days.'

'No,' Ellen said, 'my mum's having a lie in. Like I said, they're sleeping.'

Jonathan couldn't think what to say next.

They stared at each other a minute.

Ellen took a packet of cigarettes from her shirt pocket and lit one. She stood staring at Jonathan and took a long drag on her cigarette, still staring at him. She blew smoke towards him.

'I had an accident,' Jonathan said. 'That's why I'm at home.'

'I see,' said Ellen, taking another drag.

'I'd better get on.'

74

Ellen didn't reply.

'If you see my cat,' Jonathan said, 'let me know.'

He turned and made his way slowly back across the lawn towards the French windows. He could feel Ellen's eyes on his back as he went. He was tempted to turn round but resisted.

He was more convinced than ever that Ellen had killed her mother and her dog. He hadn't seen her put the dog in the hole. He just knew that she hadn't been doing 'a spot of gardening'; she had been burying Sandy.

Theodore watched from the bottom of the hedge as Jonathan returned inside. Then he turned his attention back to Ellen.

She had left the spade sticking in the ground and was now pacing in front of the patio doors, smoking her cigarette. She kept looking at the patch of soil and the hedge which separated her from Emily and Jonathan's house. She smoked the cigarette down to the filter and then tossed it onto the top of the dog's grave.

Then she went back into her house, sliding the patio doors closed behind her.

North by Northwest

Theodore approached the dog's grave and the cigarette butt that still smouldered. Sandy was buried at least two feet below the ground. He wouldn't be able to dig up the dog, and even if he did, what would he do with it then? He could hardly drag it through the hedge and drop it at Jonathan's feet.

He walked towards the house, where Ellen was now in the kitchen, vigorously washing her hands in the sink.

He made it to the wall of the house without being seen. In front of him were the sliding glass doors that opened onto the lounge. Above his head was Ellen's bedroom window.

He was standing on a patio made up of concrete paving slabs. A thousand cigarette ends littered the ground. Theodore noted that some of them had burned down to the filter.

There was a rectangle of lighter grey, measuring about six feet by four feet. Theodore noticed some dark grey marks outside this rectangle. He examined them carefully. They were charcoal. He looked closely at the bricks and mortar of the wall that flanked the sliding doors. In the small crevices, he noted particles of soot. They extended up the wall and stopped at the windowsill of Ellen's bedroom. The bottom of the windowsill was blackened.

He looked out across the lawn, to where the shed stood.

Had there been two sheds, he wondered, or had the shed been put there to replace one that had burned down. He remembered what Wally had said, *'Then one weekend he was gone. Whoosh! Just like that.'*

He looked up once more at Ellen's bedroom window and then down at the patio and the cigarette ends that lay there.

Then there was a ringing from inside the house. The telephone went straight to the answerphone.

'It's Penny. Can you answer the phone, Ellen?'

Then, 'I know you're there... Please just answer the phone. I'm starting to worry. Ellen?'

Theodore saw Ellen enter the room. He pressed himself flat against the ground; he could feel cigarette butts against his abdomen.

'Just let me speak to mum... I'm going to have to come up if you don't answer the phone Ellen... I'm worried about you.'

There was a beep. Then the doors slid open. Ellen towered over Theodore. In her hand she held a saucepan. She threw the contents at Theodore.

He was already running towards the hedge that separated the garden from Stuart's when the water hit him.

At least it's not soup, Theodore thought, as he dived through the gap in the hedge.

Stuart was in his shed. Theodore was a couple of feet away and could hear tapping coming from inside, and every so often a string of expletives.

'Rattle, rattle, tap, tap,' the shed went, and then: 'Och! Och! Mah cock's on a block... Och! Och! Mahcocksonablock.'

Theodore narrowed his eyes. I wonder what he's up to in there, he thought.

He padded down the side of the shed and into the garden. There was no sign of Hamish, the ginger tom. Theodore took the opportunity of spraying parts of the hedge and the side of the shed, expanding his territory. He had no fear of Hamish.

But suddenly there was a whirring overhead. He stopped mid-flow and looked up.

A drone was hovering two feet above him, descending on its sets of propellers.

Theodore dived sideways into the vegetable patch, just avoiding the drone as it dropped at him from out of the skies.

He was hidden by the foliage of potato plants. He could hear the drone go over head, darting up and down the rows of vegetables.

He dashed to another row and the drone descended at the same time, almost catching him with its whirring propellers whipping up the air above his head. Now's not the time for a fur-cut, thought Theodore.

He glanced up through the vegetable leaves and in the back bedroom window he saw his adversary.

Stuart's ten-year-old son Dougie was leaning out of his bedroom window, remote controller in hand, piloting the drone that hovered menacingly above Theodore, waiting for the cat's next move.

Dougie grinned with childish malevolence. To break a butterfly on a wheel was one thing; to conduct an aerial assault on a cat was a new one on Theodore.

No wonder Hamish was keeping out of sight: it was the Easter holidays...

He was going to have to make a break for it, Theodore realised, as the drone swooped low over his hiding place.

The drone came back for a second pass, its propellers clipping the tops of the plants and sending them into the air.

Theodore dashed to the edge of the vegetable patch where it joined the lawn. There was a two foot gap he would have to cross to reach the safety of the hedge.

Dougie saw the movement in the plants and sent the drone down the corridor cutting off the cat's escape.

Theodore miaowed for human intervention.

But Stuart was still tapping away and cursing in his shed; Wally was busy trying to keep his fire going, and Jonathan was back inside, probably watching the rest of *North by Northwest.*

The drone came down once more, clipping the leaves from above his head. He flattened himself against the ground.

He looked and saw the drone hovering in the air, just a few feet away, its blue and white plastic shell held up by its four whirring propellers. A red light flicked on and off on the underside of the drone: Dougie was recording the attack to enjoy later.

Theodore was fed up of running. He would make a stand. He chose his moment and dashed out onto the strip of lawn.

The drone came straight at him. Theodore jumped and struck out with one paw, aiming it in between the whirring propellers at a circular strip of plastic.

He made contact with the plastic body of the machine, sending it crashing into the side of the shed, where it fell to the ground.

Theodore dashed to the bottom of the hedge as the shed door was thrown open.

'What's going on out here,' shouted Stuart.

'My drone,' Dougie shouted down from his bedroom window. 'It crashed... Sorry!'

'You bloody tweeny sod!'

Stuart looked at the plastic toy lying on the lawn. 'It looks like you've gone and bust it. Forty quid that cost.'

'It wasn't my fault,' Dougie said. 'It was that big grey cat.'

Stuart looked around the garden. There were no cats to be seen. 'Cat, mah arse,' he said.

'But dad…' Dougie began.

'I may be mad north by northwest,' Stuart said and waved his forefinger at his son, who was his own spitting image. *'When the wind is southerly, I know a hawk from a hacksaw!'*

And with this Shakespearean quotation, he went back inside his shed and slammed the door shut behind him.

Scots in Space

Like quite a few people with overactive imaginations, Stuart McRae believed that people originated from outer space. Stuart, however, went one step further. He believed that the different races on Earth came from different planets. The Scots were from one planet, the English another.

The Scots on their home planet had limited food, so had gone in search of other planets. They had discovered Scotland and in its rich soils they had grown the oats from which they made their porridge.

He put his ideas into books: a planned series of Scottish Science Fiction featuring a band of feisty Scots who travel the universe, battling the anaemic English and other alien breeds. His first book in the series, working title: 'Scots in Space', was nearing completion and he was looking forward to the royalties pouring in. He would put the money into offshore bank accounts to make sure the English taxman couldn't get a slice of it. He was even considering opening a Swiss bank account; he admired the Swiss: they knew how to squirrel away other people's money.

In the meantime, he played househusband to two children: Dougie and Daisy. His wife, Leslie, worked for a bank in the centre of York and made enough money for them to live in reasonable comfort – just until his first book was published, he told Leslie. Then they would leave England, return to Scotland and buy a castle by a loch, and Leslie would not have to work again.

It was just a matter of time before the literary world would bow to his pen.

He bashed another paragraph into his laptop:

The Scots of Scaramanga had long lived under the oppressive oligarchy of the English tyrants. Then, one day, a man emerged who would in time sow the seed of discontent and begin the uprising that would bring down the oligarchs. He was the chosen Scot. His name was Hamish McHaddock. Hamish would bring down the oligarchical governance that oppressed the people of Scaramanga.

Stuart liked the word *oligarch*. He read out loud his latest paragraph, emphasizing the *arch* of oligarch each time the word cropped up.

Hamish McHaddock, the hero of his book, was a younger, more handsome, more eloquent version of himself. His adversary, William Weakbladder, was drawn from his neighbour over the hedge, Wally. Though set in outer space, his novel was firmly rooted in Acomb.

He heard Leslie call his name from outside the shed.

For another minute he continued to bash away at the keyboard. Then the shed door swung open. Leslie was standing, arms folded across her chest.

Leslie's chest was quite formidable. It was what had drawn Stuart to her in their early days of courtship, when he had been the steward on the early morning Edinburgh-bound train that she took each morning. He had impressed her by his knowledge of the Scottish bard. He had quoted Burns to her as he poured her coffee each morning. It had been Leslie who had eventually plucked up the courage to ask if the lyrical train guard would like to meet up after work one day –

just for a wee dram. It was Stuart's gift of the gab that won her heart.

Leslie's chest had been what had drawn Stuart to his future wife, but what had once been objects of adoration for Stuart had become objects of practical use with the birth of their two children and off limits to Stuart and then after breast-feeding had been done with, they had never returned to their former role.

'Haven't you forgotten something?' Leslie said, her arms still folded across her chest.

Stuart's intergalactic War and Peace was going to have to wait, he realised, saving his work with a control's'.

'Have I forgotten something?'

'You're supposed to be taking the kids to parkour,' Leslie said.

'I was just finishing this wee paragraph,' Stuart said.

'Well, your wee paragraph can wait.'

'Why can't you take them?'

'Because it's your job to take them,' Leslie said. 'And I'm supposed to be working. You know that.'

'I don't see why they cannot just jump about the garden.'

'Look: we've already paid for parkour. The kids have been inside all day, playing on their phones, and you went and dug over most of the lawn so you could plant vegetables, so they can't very well play in the garden.'

'All right, all right, I'll take them.'

A mobile phone began to ring from within the house and Leslie dashed back inside.

Stuart shut his shed door and entering the lounge he heard Leslie snap into her phone, 'Just power off, count to ten and then start it up again… If it still doesn't work, call me back.'

The garden and shed now quiet, Theodore ventured out from the bottom of the hedge.

There was still no sign of Hamish, so he took the opportunity to empty his bowels in Stuart's vegetable patch. He kicked some soil over and then gazed at the back of Stuart's house.

Leslie was pacing in front of the lounge window, her mobile phone in her hand. She was tapping frantically away at the screen.

Leslie was a secret gambling addict. What had started as a bit of harmless fun at the end of the working day had become an all-consuming obsession. At night she would lie in bed clicking away while her husband read a chapter of his book. Stuart wasn't aware that she had squandered most of their savings. But she knew, with a little bit of luck, she would eventually make it all back and more besides.

She used a website called Doggo Bingo. Doggo was a Yorkshire terrier with spinning pound coins for eyes and a pink tongue that slithered saliva. He wore a top hat with a pink band. A playing card stuck out from the band: the jack of diamonds.

Theodore watched her waste another hundred pounds in less than two minutes on Doggo Bingo, her fingers jabbing away at the screen of her iPhone, her forehead creased.

Humans would be better off without hands. Theodore glanced at his paws and then back to Leslie's fingers, still jabbing away at the screen of her iPhone. All pad and no claw, thought Theodore.

Bad Friday

Emily was not in a good mood when she got home.

It was Good Friday, and during her lunch break she had gone out to M&S and bought a whole salmon for dinner, as she was traditionally minded enough to avoid meat on this day. She left the plastic bag containing the fish in her car when she returned to the soft furnishing store for her afternoon shift.

The shop's owner was on a three week holiday in Thailand and Emily had been left in charge. The widow of a local fish and chip tycoon had entered the shop with the intention of furnishing a dozen properties she had bought on the Terry's site in York, now named the Chocolate Works, and was going to let them out. Emily had widened her eyes when the woman had taken out her purse and paid in cash. Almost twenty thousand pounds.

How many fish and chips did you have to sell to make that sort of money? How many hours would she have to spend working in a shop to make that sort of money?

The banks were closed as it was a Bank Holiday and wouldn't be open again until Tuesday. She knew there were such things as night safes but was unsure how they worked. So, rather than leaving the money in the till overnight, she put it in her handbag. They wouldn't count it until the banks reopened on Tuesday anyway, so what difference did it make?

It had been a sunny afternoon, and when she got back in her car, it stank of fish. She drove home with her windows down.

Now the plastic bag containing the smelly salmon sat next to her handbag containing twenty thousand pounds on the kitchen side.

She removed the salmon and slid it into a dish. She took out a container of mashed potato from the fridge. She removed the cardboard sleeve. She took a knife from the drawer and began to stab the plastic cover, the knife going through the contents and stabbing the wooden counter surface below. She didn't notice; her attention was focussed on her handbag.

She would take the cash into the bank on Tuesday morning. What did it matter, a few days?

While she was sorting out dinner, Jonathan came into the kitchen. He sat down on a stool and rested his crutches in the corner. 'Something smells a bit fishy,' he said.

'That'll be the fish,' Emily said. 'So what have you been doing all day?'

Jonathan spread his palms, wondering where to begin. 'I think she killed the dog today,' he said.

He pointed at the back door and what lay beyond. 'First she did in her mother, and now she's gone and killed the dog.'

'Oh, come off it,' said Emily, arms folded. 'People don't go killing their mothers and dogs in the middle of the afternoon. Not in Acomb they don't...'

'But it happened,' Jonathan said. 'I'm sure of it. Both me and Theodore saw the dog jumping up in the window. Then the barking stopped. Then it was quiet. And then afterwards the curtains were snapped closed again.'

'Have you been drinking?'

'No,' Jonathan said. 'Well, maybe a beer or two...'

Emily raised her eyebrows.

'Look I'm not drunk. But I do think she's done something to the dog... And her mother too.'

'You really expect me to believe that some old woman behind, who I have never seen for that matter, has been murdered by her daughter? And now her dog's been killed?'

'She was in the garden. She had dug a hole. I reckon she had buried the dog. Or maybe even her mother's head. I never saw her putting anything in the ground. She'd already covered it over. But I'm sure she's buried something in the garden.'

'I've heard enough,' Emily said.

'And the curtains haven't been opened all today,' Jonathan went on.

'Give it a rest,' Emily said. 'I've had a crap day at work. I don't need this as soon as I get in.'

She turned and went over to the back door. She looked across the garden to the house behind.

'Well, they're open now... And the television's on. You can see the light flickering.'

Jonathan got to his feet and crossed to the back door. 'You're right. She's gone and opened them, and she must have turned the TV on to make it look like her mum's in there watching it.'

'Look,' Emily said, 'if you really are concerned about the old lady, why don't you just ask the daughter next time you see her?'

'Ask her what? Did you kill your mother?'

'You ask how her mother is.'

'I will,' Jonathan said. 'Tomorrow... I'll ask her how her mother is. See what she says.'

'She was just doing a spot of gardening,' Emily said. 'Maybe you should do something about our garden. The lawn needs cutting. It'll take your mind off all this murder nonsense...'

'I can't do the garden,' Jonathan said. 'Not with my foot.'

'Well, *I* don't know anything about gardening, and I'm not going to start learning now.'

'We could get a gardener.'

'Gardeners cost money and I don't see you earning any sitting there.'

'I'm on sick leave,' Jonathan protested. 'I'm still being paid…'

'Enough about gardens and dead mothers,' Emily said. 'You haven't even asked me about my day.'

'How was your day?' Jonathan said.

Emily shook her head. 'I'm going to get changed now. When I come back down I don't want to hear any more about dead dogs and murdered mothers.'

Theodore watched as she went upstairs taking her handbag with her. He followed.

When Theodore entered the bedroom, Emily was sitting on the edge of the bed. Banknotes fanned out across the duvet. Theodore jumped up onto the bed and stared at the money.

The concept of money baffled him. It was a difficult concept for most humans to get a grip on. You work so that you can gain money, so that you can sleep in a bed, eat food and maybe, if you are lucky, have one or two weeks' holiday from the tedium of work. To a cat's mind, those things should be a basic requirement of existence, not something that required eight hours labour a day.

Emily too wondered at the point of it all. She stared into Theodore's eyes and began to stroke him.

Theodore felt the tension release from her as she stroked him and a faraway look appeared in her face.

Emily is lying on a deckchair in front of a five star hotel. She is wearing a black and white striped swimsuit by Whistles, sunglasses by Fendi and hat by Melissa Odabash.

Waiters wander around with trays of drinks. She lowers her sunglasses and gazes across at the other hotel guests. None of them look like they do a hard day's work and neither does she.

She gets up and pads over the golden sand. The sun glistens on the turquoise blue of the sea.

A young bronzed man calls out to her. He looks like a young George Clooney crossed with Brad Pitt. He is standing in front of a convertible car.

'Well, are you going to jump in?' George/Brad says. 'I thought we could have a romantic dinner and then dance away the night at a little club I know.'

'Sounds fun,' Emily says. 'But I'm not really dressed.'

'I'm sure we could call in and get you a little something on the way… It's on me.'

'Well, if you insist,' Emily says, walking over to the waiting George/Brad.

She lets him give her a little kiss on the cheek before she climbs into the car, George/Brad holding the door for her while she gets in.

In the distance a telephone rings.

Then George/Brad says, 'Are you going to get that?'

But it wasn't George/Brad's voice. It was Jonathan's.

'Telephone!' he shouted again from downstairs.

Emily stopped stroking Theodore and began to gather up the banknotes. She pushed them back into a plastic envelope and put the money into the drawer of her bedside locker. She then rushed downstairs, the telephone still ringing insistently from the table in the hall. She knew who it was; only her mother called the landline.

Theodore stayed on the bed a minute. He stared at the closed drawer of the bedside cabinet. He then looked at the tower of paperbacks stacked on top, their spines facing him. He read the capitalised titles:

TOO GOOD TO BE TRUE
THE MAN ON THE BUS
THE BETRAYAL
THE GIRL YOU LOST
NO KISS GOODBYE
EAT, PRAY, LOVE
NO COMING BACK
THE NEW LIFE

He noted that she had yet to read *The New Life* by Nobel-prize-winning Turkish author Orhan Pamuk, as the spine was uncreased; either that or she had started and soon given up. He furrowed his brow, blinked his eyes and then jumped down from the bed.

Emily was still on the phone to her mother.

'But it's only Easter,' she said, 'won't it be too cold for a barbecue.' She was then silent as she listened to her mum Trish speaking.

Then: 'Well, if he insists…'

A minute's silence, then: 'No, he's still resting his foot… I've really just got in.'

Theodore soon lost interest in the one-sided conversation. He padded across the hall and slipped into the kitchen.

A minute later Emily entered the lounge.

'My parents invited us over to Acaster Mildew on Sunday for Easter lunch,' she said to the back of Jonathan's head. 'But as you are not mobile, they are coming over here instead.'

'So you're cooking?'

'No,' Emily said. 'My dad's already bought the food in and he's insisting that he wants to cook... Surf and turf.'

'Surf and turf?'

'He likes to do it on the barbecue. Prawns for starter, then lamb cutlets. Barbecued pear and brandy snap surprise for pudding. It's sort of an Easter tradition.'

'But we don't have a barbecue.'

'He's bringing one over, along with the food.'

'I guess that's all right then.'

Emily said. 'I'd better put dinner on. It's already quarter to eight.'

She entered the kitchen.

'Theo!' she screamed.

Theodore was on top of the salmon, wolfing down the pink fish flesh. He stopped and jumped down onto the floor. He dashed at the backdoor, but then remembered there was no cat flap. He turned round and dashed past Emily, who was standing in front of the remains of the salmon.

Emily screamed, and then whimpered from behind her hands which she held over her face, 'That was our dinner...'

The Cat Who Knew Too Much

Emily slept through her alarm on Easter Saturday. She was working that day and left the house without saying more than two words to either Jonathan or Theodore.

Theodore ate some biscuits left over from the day before and then went back upstairs.

He settled on the back bedroom window. He could see Ellen in her kitchen, emptying the kitchen bin. She opened the back door and carried the bin liner over to the black wheelie bin. She threw it in and was about to return inside when Stuart appeared at the boundary hedge.

'Got a spare ciggie?' he shouted over at her.

'Are you ever going to buy any?' Ellen said, walking towards him.

She handed over a cigarette and noticed Stuart staring down at her chest. She was wearing one of her father's old shirts, three buttons undone. She knew that Stuart fancied her. He didn't try to hide it. Although he was pushing forty he was handsome in a virile sort of way. Besides, there weren't any other men who had ever shown any interest in her.

'I've a shelf I need putting up,' Ellen said, lighting his cigarette. 'In my bedroom.'

She lit a cigarette for herself.

'I can put a shelf up for you,' Stuart said. 'I'll bring my drill round later.'

'Well, I'm about to have a bath,' Ellen said, blowing smoke provocatively at Stuart. 'Give us an hour or so.'

'Righty-ho,' said Stuart. 'What about your mum? Won't all the drilling disturb her?'

'Don't worry about her,' Ellen said. 'She was up late. She'll be dead to the world.'

'Whatever you say,' Stuart said. 'I'll be round later.'

'I'll leave the back door unlocked. Just come straight up and I'll be waiting.'

'Not a problem.'

'And don't forget your drill,' Ellen said with a smile.

Theodore was distracted by a blur of black and white at the kitchen door. It was a magpie. He watched as it flapped about inside the kitchen. Another magpie stood guard on the edge of the overgrown lawn.

Theodore turned his attention back to Ellen. She was walking back towards her house. Stuart was staring at her back, at her rear end to be precise.

As Ellen reached the back door, the bird flew out of the house. She flapped her arms at the bird. 'Get out of it,' she shouted after it.

Theodore watched from the bedroom window as the magpie disappeared into the branches of an apple tree in Geoffrey's garden.

Ellen closed the kitchen door and went upstairs to have a bath. Theodore jumped down from the windowsill and trotted downstairs.

Jonathan looked out of the French windows at the house that overlooked his. The curtains in both back bedrooms were open.

He remembered that he was going to confront his neighbour Ellen about her mother and the dog; he decided to put it off. Maybe Emily was right. He was just reading too much into it.

'Fancy watching a film?' he said to Theodore.

The cat was strutting up and down in front of the French windows, miaowing from time to time, already wanting to be out in the garden.

'The Man Who Knew Too Much,' Jonathan said, waving the plastic box at Theodore. 'We might as well give it a go.'

He got to his feet on his crutches and managed to slot the DVD into the player.

Theodore looked at the television screen.

An American couple, played by James Stewart and Doris Day, and their young son, played by Christopher Olsen, are sitting on the back seat of a bus, travelling through a busy Marrakesh market place. The boy spots a camel through the side window of the bus. 'Oh, look, a camel,' he says.

And the three of them turn to look at it through the rear window of the bus.

Theodore looked through the rear window of the bus but there was no camel to be seen.

Soon, a Frenchman makes their acquaintance.

The boy says to the soon-to-be-murdered Frenchman, 'If you ever get hungry, our garden back home is full of snails. We tried everything to get rid of them. We never thought of a Frenchman!'

And they all laugh.

Theodore turned from the television screen and peered through the French windows. He glimpsed the red cap of Wally, standing over a smouldering fire. He looked across at the house behind. He saw Ellen in her bedroom. She wasn't alone.

On the television screen, Doris Day sang of being a little girl and asking her mother about her future, and her mother replying with, *'Que Sera, Sera'.* What will be, will be.

Jonathan turned from the screen and through the French windows he looked across at Ellen's bedroom window. He saw Ellen's face appear in the window. She looked across at him and mouthed:

'When I was just a young woman
I took a pillow
From my mum's bed.
You asked if I held it
Until she was dead?
What do you think I said?

Jonathan looked at the television screen and then back through the French windows up at Ellen's bedroom window. Ellen's face was close to the window. She sang the garbled chorus:

'Que paso, paso
Whatever I did, I did
The past is not yours to know
Que paso, paso
What happened is so... is so.'

Another face then came into focus from the shadows of the room. It was coated in red hairs with red cheeks to match. It was Stuart. His face moved forwards and backwards behind Ellen, in and out of focus.

Then Ellen, her cheeks pink, her mousey-brown hair hanging across her face, sang:

'When poor Sandy wouldn't shut up
You ask me, neighbour
You ask with a sigh
Did I throttle her?
Poor little Sandy
Did the pooch have to die?

Then, from behind her, Stuart joined in:

> 'Que paso, paso
> Whatever she did, she did
> The past is not yours to know
> Que paso, paso
> What happened is so… is so.'

Then Ellen sang:

> 'Well, I've got concerns of my own
> I ask my conscience
> What should I do?
> Shall I confess all?
> Tell the police?
> Why, they'd have a ball
> If only they knew!'

Ellen's face was now pressed to the window, her cheeks pink, as she mouthed out the words:

> 'Que paso, paso
> Whatever I did, I did
> The past is not yours to know
> Que paso, paso
> What happened is so… is so.'

Jonathan managed to look away. He looked down at Theodore, who was sitting in front of the French windows.

Theodore turned to him and miaowed what sounded like: 'Que paso, paso.'

'Not you, as well,' Jonathan cried and threw a cushion at the cat.

Theodore darted behind the sofa.

Jonathan looked back up at the window.

Ellen's mouth was wide, her face pressed up against the glass. Stuart was behind her, working his way frantically to a climax. They both stared down at Jonathan and sang out:

'Que paso, paso
Whatever I did, I did.'

Jonathan put his hands to his face, covering his eyes, as Ellen, Stuart and Theodore, from somewhere behind the sofa, all sang at the tops of their voices:

Que paso, paso
What happened is so… is so
Que paso, paso!'

When he opened his eyes, the curtains in Ellen's bedroom had been pulled shut and Theodore was sitting once more in front of the French windows.

From outside he heard a woman call out, 'Stuart! Stuart! Are you out here?'

Rogue Window Cleaner

Nigel Bates returned that afternoon.

Jonathan, shaken by what he had seen in Ellen's window, was actually pleased to see him. He got up from the sofa and opened the French windows.

Theodore darted through the open windows and out onto the lawn.

'Just wanted to make sure there were no more smears,' Nigel said, watching the cat make for the hedge at the back of the garden.

'They look fine to me,' Jonathan said. 'Has work not picked up?'

'Still a bit slow,' Nigel said. 'I've started telling people to call me Nigel now. I'm starting to like it. Norman was a bit old fashioned when you think about it.'

'That's good, Nigel.'

'I'm going to change it officially by dead pool.'

Jonathan knew that Nigel meant deed poll but didn't bother to correct him; he had something else on his mind. 'You mentioned the house behind the first time you came round,' Jonathan said. 'Terrible business, you said.'

'I remember it well,' Nigel said. He took off his beanie and scratched his head. 'Not something you forget in a hurry. Must have been ten years ago.'

'What actually happened?'

'There was a fire, wasn't there? Shed went up in flames with him inside. They say a petrol can had been leaking fumes.'

'But what caused it to suddenly burst into flames?'

'That's the funny thing. The word was that the young girl had been smoking out of her window. Then lobbed her fag end out, and that's what did it. An accident like.'

'Then what happened? What happened to the girl?'

'Nothing, I don't think. She was just a young lass. It was an accident, wasn't it? They took pity on her.'

Jonathan stared at the house behind. 'I think Ellen might have had another accident...'

Nigel stared at him at moment. 'You're kidding. You only get one dad. You can't kill him twice.'

'Not her dad this time,' Jonathan said. 'This time she's killed her mum. But it wasn't an accident.'

'Well, she should be put away then. She's not a young girl anymore. You can't just go round killing your parents...'

'I know. But I can't prove anything... I think she killed her in her bedroom. Smothered her with her pillow. I didn't see it, mind you. But the old woman was screaming; then she was quiet. And then I haven't seen or heard anything from her since.'

Nigel stared at Jonathan, his face vacant.

'I think she did it for the money,' Jonathan went on. 'For the house... The last thing she cried was: "It's going to the dogs!" So Ellen thought she wasn't going to inherit anything.'

Nigel continued to look expressionlessly at Jonathan. He didn't say anything.

'You don't believe me, do you?' Jonathan said.

Nigel turned and looked at the house behind. 'The windows look like they could do with a clean.'

Jonathan's eyes widened. 'That's it,' he cried, clapping his hands together. 'You've got ladders. You could take them round and do the windows. While you're there, you could look in the windows and see if you can see her mum. That's her bedroom on the right.'

'You can't just go round and clean someone's windows unless they ask you to.'

'What if we wait till she goes out? Then you go round and wash the windows…'

'But I won't get paid…'

'I'll pay you,' Jonathan said.

'Well, as long as I'm not going to get into trouble.'

'Come on. Let's go upstairs. From the back bedroom we'll be able to see when she goes out. Then you head round.'

Ten minutes later they were in the back bedroom. They could see through the sliding doors Ellen working at the dining room table. After an hour of waiting, they saw her gather up a wad of brown envelopes, grab a hoodie and make her way out of the back door.

From the bottom of the hedge, Theodore watched her leave. Ten minutes later he saw Nigel walk along the side of the house, carrying his ladders over his shoulder.

He put them up so they reached the bottom of Tessa's bedroom window. He disappeared and then returned a couple of minutes later with a bucket. He then began to climb the ladder, the bucket in his left hand.

Theodore turned round and looked back at his own house. He could see Jonathan in the bedroom window, a pair of binoculars held to his face.

He turned back to Ellen's house. Nigel was near the top of the ladder. The curtains had been left half open. He peered into the darkened room.

Suddenly Ellen appeared round the corner of the house. 'What are you doing?' she cried.

Without waiting for a reply, she rushed at the ladder and pushed it over.

The ladder landed on the paving stones with a clatter. Nigel landed with a thump. The empty bucket rolled across the patio and came to a rest against the sliding glass doors.

Nigel cried out in pain. 'My leg! My leg!' he screamed, holding his leg. 'I've broken my leg.'

Theodore looked at Nigel's leg and noticed it was bent at an impossible angle.

'Call an ambulance,' Nigel shouted. 'Please!'

Ellen took her mobile phone from her jeans pocket. 'Hello! Hello! Yes… Police… I've just stopped someone trying to break into my house…'

Jonathan was also on his phone, calling an ambulance.

It was an hour before a police officer knocked on Jonathan's door. By which time Nigel had been taken to hospital in an ambulance, accompanied by another police officer.

'I'm Police Constable Pigeon,' the police officer said. 'You can call me Gary.'

'You'd better come in,' Jonathan said.

He made his way through to the lounge and PC Gary Pigeon followed.

When they were both sitting down, Gary said, 'I believe you are a witness to the attempted break in at 64 Constantine Crescent. The house behind…'

'Yes but no,' Jonathan said. 'I mean I saw what happened, but it was not an attempted break in.'

'Not a break in? Well, what was he doing up there? The bucket he had with him didn't have a trace of water in it.'

'He was trying to see inside…'

'A voyeur? Are you sure? It's more likely he was scoping the house. Waited until she'd gone out, and then thought he'd have a quick look. See if there was anything worth nicking.'

'No, it wasn't like that. He was checking if her mother was alive…'

'I'll stop you there,' Gary said. 'I don't think you know who you're dealing with. The suspect gave us a false name when he was arrested. Said he was called Nigel. But when we checked his driving licence, it was Norman. And then we did a quick look on our system and it turns out that he's not even registered.'

'Registered?'

'Yes, registered. Registered to be a window cleaner.'

'Do you have to be registered to be a window cleaner?'

'Of course, you do,' Gary said. 'We can't have just anyone putting up ladders and peeping through people's windows, can we?'

'I didn't know.'

'If you didn't need to be registered, anybody could set themselves up and go peering through people's windows.'

'I wouldn't,' Jonathan said. 'I suffer from vertigo.'

'Well, maybe not you,' Gary said. 'But this Norman, he's an unsavoury character. He's a maverick. A wild card. A rogue window cleaner.'

'I didn't realise,' Jonathan said. 'I'd never heard of rogue window cleaners.'

'They are anarchists,' Gary said. 'You probably don't remember the Window Cleaning Wars of the 1980s.'

'I'm afraid I don't.'

'It was a turf war. Too many of them going for too few windows. Encroaching on each other's territories. There was fighting in the streets. Blades drawn. A lot of broken windows. Very unpleasant business.'

'I had no idea.'

'Thatcher tried to sort them out. But the NUWC, that's the National Union of Window Cleaners, was too powerful even for her. The NUWC organised a national strike and they all put their blades down. People had to endure dirty windows for weeks. They refer to it as the Summer of the Window Cleaners' Discontent.'

'I think I might have heard of that.'

Gary stood up and began to pace in front of the French windows. 'You will have heard of the Great Uprising of the Window Cleaners.'

Jonathan nodded.

'It was following the introduction of the window tax in 1696,' Gary said. 'They taxed people on the number of windows they had. So people began to brick up their windows. Now, what do you think is going to happen?'

'Less windows?' Jonathan guessed.

'Less windows to clean. Who's that going to affect?'

'The window cleaners?'

'That's right,' Gary said. 'The window cleaners. They weren't happy at all. There were protests. It began in the north. They ended up marching on London. Others joining as they approached the capital. Parliament sent the army to meet them. There was a great battle.

'That was all a long time ago,' Gary said. 'But you bear in mind: always be wary of window cleaners. Be *very* wary of window cleaners.'

'I will,' Jonathan said nodding. 'What's going to happen to Nigel? I mean Norman.'

'He'll be charged with unsolicited window cleaning, I imagine. Soon as he's allowed out of hospital. We can't do much till then, but as soon as he's out, he'll feel the full weight of the law.'

'I see.'

'I think your cat wants to come in,' Gary said nodding at the French windows. 'And I'd better be off. I've got a lot of paperwork to do because of this.'

Jonathan looked and saw Theodore sitting in front of the French windows. The cat miaowed to be let in.

'I'll see myself out,' Gary said, and saw himself out.

Jonathan realised it was probably for the best that he hadn't said anything to Gary to implicate himself. He got to his feet and let Theodore back in.

Voyer!

When Emily got home that evening, Jonathan told her what he'd seen that afternoon. 'She was having sex in front of her bedroom window,' he said. 'Doggy-style.'

'Are you sure?' Emily said shaking her head.

'Well, he was behind her, and she was moving backwards and forwards.'

'No,' Emily said, shaking her head. 'I meant, are you sure you're not just imagining it, like the murdered mum and the dead dog.'

'I saw them at it, I tell you. They were at it like... Well, like dogs. Her and that Scottish man.'

'Yes, you said.'

'And then she knocked Nigel off his ladder and he's been taken to hospital.'

'Who's Nigel?' Emily said, staring out through the French windows.

'He's the window cleaner,' Jonathan said. 'A rogue window cleaner...'

Emily stared outside. 'There's a card in the bedroom window,' she said, squinting

There was a rectangle of white paper stuck to Ellen's bedroom window. It read:

VOYER!

'It says voyeur,' said Emily.

Jonathan got to his feet and went over to the French windows. 'I don't think that's how you spell voyeur.'

'She knows that you've been watching her,' Emily said.

'She made sure I was watching her.'

'You didn't have to sit there and watch.'

'I didn't want to have to sit there and watch.'

'You are obsessed with her.'

'I am not obsessed by her.'

'You are.'

'I'm not.'

'I am going to get changed now,' Emily said. 'When I come back down, I don't want to hear any more about her. I'm sick of it.'

Then Emily left the room, leaving Jonathan standing in front of the French windows, holding himself up by his sticks.

He stared at the rectangle of white paper. Then he looked at the next window. A light was on in Tessa's bedroom.

A figure was silhouetted against the sunflower curtains. It looked like Tessa. It was her hair, or at least her wig. She was sitting up in bed, watching television. From time to time, she raised a bottle to her mouth and drank. So Tessa was alive after all.

Jonathan shook his head. He reached for the package of tablets on the coffee table. He removed the folded sheet of paper they came with and began to read the long list of possible side effects.

Theodore followed Emily upstairs.

Emily took from her handbag, several more clear plastic bags of rolled-up money and emptied then across her duvet.

'Oh, Theo,' Emily said. 'Look at all this money. There's thousands here. And that's just today's takings.'

She began to stroke Theodore with one hand and with her other she stroked the money.

'Imagine what we could do with this,' she murmured, closing her eyes.

Emily is wearing a dress by Alice Temperly. She is carrying a Mulberry handbag. On her wrist she is wearing a watch by Larsson & Jennings.

She is standing in front of a roulette table. In front of her are hundreds of brightly-coloured chips in several cylindrical towers. The wheel comes to a stop and more chips are pushed her way by the croupier.

'It looks like you can't help but win today,' a handsome man in a suit standing next to her says and smiles a bleached white smile.

'It certainly appears that way,' Emily says. 'I don't know what I'm going to do with so much money…'

'You could buy a boat with all that dough,' the man says and laughs.

A little later, Emily is dressed in an Eres Diagramme one-shoulder swimsuit and sunglasses from Oliver Peoples Sayer.

She is standing on the deck of a speedboat. The man, who is called Carlos and bears a striking resemblance to Antonio Banderas, is at the controls, propelling the boat across a bay of choppy azure. Carlos is wearing just a pair of silky white shorts by Prada and sunglasses by Dolce & Gabbana. His body is burnt caramel. The sun shines down from a cloudless sky.

'This is such fun!' Emily says laughing and Carlos laughs too.

They pass very close to a rowing boat. Jonathan is struggling with a pair of oars and not making much progress. His hair is damp with sweat and stuck to his forehead. He is wearing supermarket own brand t-shirt and shorts.

As Emily and Carlos pass, a tidal wave created by the speedboat almost capsizes Jonathan.

'I think I might have splashed that pasty-looking Englishman,' Carlos says.

'Don't worry about him, Carlos,' Emily laughs. 'He's just my ex-boyfriend...'

She laughs so hard, her eyes are closed.

She opened her eyes to be faced by Theodore's wide green stare.

'Oh, Theodore,' Emily said, returning from her reveries. 'There's nothing wrong with dreaming. Life can be so tedious. What have we but our dreams?'

That night Jonathan and Emily watched a film set in San Francisco, featuring a detective who follows and then becomes obsessed with an attractive woman. It was called *Basic Instinct*.

This seems familiar, thought Theodore. He stretched and got down from the sofa.

From the back bedroom window Theodore watched as Geoffrey let Lucy out, for her fifteen minutes of freedom, before he locked up for the night.

The Labrador went straight over to the hedge they shared with Ellen. She began scratting at the ground in front of the hedge, concentrating her efforts at a spot where the vegetation was sparsest.

She dug furiously, sending dirt into the air behind her. Then she put her head to the ground and Theodore saw it emerge on the other side of the hedge. She then squeezed the rest of her body through the gap she had made. She was in Ellen's garden.

She ran over to the flowerbed, where Sandy the Shih Zhu was buried, and began to dig.

Theodore glanced over at the back of Ellen's house. A dark human-shaped shadow appeared in the kitchen window.

Easter Sunday

Emily woke early on Easter Sunday. Within minutes she realised what day it was and her mind turned to chocolate.

Theodore was sleeping by her side. On her other side, Jonathan lay. He had managed to make his way upstairs the night before. He was still sleeping, snoring. He still wore the boot on his injured foot. It lay on top of the duvet.

After petting Theodore for some minutes, Emily poked Jonathan in the shoulder until he stirred. 'I got you an egg,' she said, placing the chocolate egg on his chest.

'An egg?' Jonathan said, rubbing his eyes.

'I know you liked minty chocolate.'

'That's very kind,' Jonathan said. 'I'm afraid I wasn't able to get you one... What with being housebound.'

'You didn't get me an egg?'

'I couldn't get to the shop to get you one.'

'Well, you'd better be prepared to share that one.'

'I'm sorry.'

'It doesn't matter really,' Emily said, but her tone of disappointment said it did.

'I'll get you one,' Jonathan said. 'Soon as I'm back on my feet.'

'Well, at least I can have a lie in,' Emily said. 'It is Sunday after all.'

Theodore miaowed from her side of the bed. It might be Sunday. He still needed feeding though, and chocolate eggs, especially minty ones, were not high on his list of favourite breakfast items.

Emily rolled over and hugged him to her.

'Yes, Theo,' she said. 'We can have a lie in together.'

Not quite the response Theodore wanted. He miaowed at her again; then crawled out from her grasp.

At that moment there came a deep rumbling from the back of the house.

'What's that?' Emily said.

'Sounds like a tractor,' said Jonathan.

'Or a tank,' said Emily.

'It must be right outside.'

He got out of bed and grabbing his crutches, crossed the landing to the back bedroom. 'It's the old guy from next door. He's cutting his lawn.'

'But it's not even eight o'clock...'

An hour later, Emily opened the bedroom curtains. That was when she saw the dead Labrador on the verge in front of their house.

'Jonathan,' she screamed.

A minute later, Jonathan approached their bedroom window. He looked out and swore; then said, 'He's only gone and parked his Audi on the flowers she planted. That's not very neighbourly.'

'No, not the car,' Emily said. 'Down there.'

Jonathan peered down and saw the dead dog on the verge, and he knew straightaway that it was Geoffrey's dog. 'It must have got run over,' he said, not so sure.

'Yes, it must have. You can't just leave it there. You're going to have to do something about it.'

'I'm not too sure what to do about it.'

'Well, you need to find out whose dog it is and then tell them to shift it. My parents are coming over later... We can't have a dead dog in front of the house. Whatever would they think?'

'I think it belongs to the blind man in the bungalow behind,' Jonathan said. 'He's not going to be happy.'

'A guide dog,' Emily said. 'That makes it even worse.'

Jonathan made his way downstairs.

He opened the front door and walked over to the dead dog. It still wore its harness. The silver identity tag attached to its collar confirmed that it was Lucy.

He looked up and down the street. There was no one around. He could hear Wally still cutting his lawn. He approached Wally's front door and knocked.

His wife Marjorie answered it.

'There's a dead dog on the verge,' he said.

'I'd better go and get Wally,' Marjorie said, peering past Jonathan. 'He'll know what to do.'

Jonathan smelled home baking coming from inside the house; then the front door closed.

A minute later Wally emerged from the side of his house. He crossed over to where the dog lay and knelt down. 'It's dead,' he said.

His eyes were moist. He blew his nose on his handkerchief.

'It's Geoffrey's dog. His guide dog. Hasn't had it a year.'

'Who's going to tell him?'

'I'll go and get him,' Wally said.

Jonathan sat down on his front wall and waited. He stared at the white Audi parked on the grass verge opposite his house and the flowers flattened below its tyres.

He heard a door creak behind him. He turned and saw Theodore saunter out of the front door. He must have left it ajar. He couldn't be bothered trying to get the cat back inside. Instead he watched as the cat approached the dead dog.

Theodore carried out a cursory examination of the crime scene.

He immediately noted the soil on the dog's paws, where she had been digging in the flowerbed.

There was dried blood around an ear and around her nostrils, the result of a single blow. Not from a passing vehicle but from the back of a spade.

He then examined the verge in front of the body. He saw two parallel lines, a paw's width wide and four cat paces apart, impressed in the grass. The lines started from the footpath and ended in deeper ruts, where the wheelie bin had been pulled over so its contents could be deposited onto the grass.

Theodore looked back to the point where the wheelie bin had been pulled onto the verge. It had come from further around Constantine Crescent, and not from York Road.

Ten minutes later, Jonathan watched as Geoffrey and Wally approached.

Geoffrey was wearing a navy blue dressing gown and brown suede slippers. He tapped a white stick in front of him.

'She's right here,' Wally said. 'Just to your left. Two feet away.'

'I'm not blind,' Geoffrey said.

'You're not?'

'I am visually impaired.' Geoffrey retracted his stick with a click of a button, so that it looked like a little white truncheon and then knelt down on the footpath beside Lucy. He moved his hands over the dog. He stroked her for some minutes.

'I'll take her to the vet's Tuesday morning,' Wally said. 'Leave it to me.'

Geoffrey didn't say anything. He stroked Lucy.

'They won't be open tomorrow, it being Easter Monday,' Wally said.

Geoffrey got to his feet. 'She never came back in last night,' he said finally. 'I let her out but she never came back. I looked all over for her... Must have got out of the garden. It's not like her at all.'

'Must have got hit by a car.'

Wally now looked across at Steve's Audi parked on the verge in front of Linda's house and shook his head slowly from side to side.

'I'll phone the guide dogs on Tuesday,' Geoffrey said. He clicked a button and his stick extended back to the ground. 'I'm sure they'll soon be able to sort something out. A replacement...'

From below Jonathan's dark blue Volvo, parked on the driveway, Theodore looked from the dead dog to its owner. Geoffrey wore his mirrored sunglasses. The sunglasses hid his eyes. They hid his feelings. They gave nothing away.

Theodore watched as Geoffrey tapped his way back along the street. Jonathan went back inside the house and Wally left but shortly returned with a blue tarpaulin. He lifted the dead dog onto the tarpaulin; then folded it over. He carried the dog away.

A minute later, from the front door of the house next door, Steve appeared, his golf bag in his hand. While he struggled with his bag and the door, Charlie the Chihuahua shot out. Steve put his golf bag in the boot of his car. He looked for a moment at the fat little dog darting about the street. He looked up at the bedroom curtains of his house that were closed. Then he got in his car and drove off.

In the house opposite, Theodore saw the Venetian blinds snap back to the horizontal, and knew that Linda, the neighbour opposite, had been watching the proceedings.

Then he made his way along the side of the house. He squeezed below the gate and was in the back garden. He was shortly on top of Wally's shed roof: his favoured surveillance spot.

Stuart had been up early, hiding little foil-wrapped chocolate eggs in his garden while his wife Leslie had a lie in.

Theodore heard him call to his children: 'Dougie! Daisy! I believe the Wee Scottie Bunny has been.'

'Tell us the story of the Wee Scottie Bunny, please daddy,' Daisy said.

'Do we have to?' Dougie said.

'Pleeaaase.'

'All right,' Stuart said and clapped his hands together. 'It was a Sunday, an Easter Sunday like today, and Jesus had been dead a few days. The Romans had put him in a cave and rolled a big rock across the entrance to the cave. And this big old rock was egg-shaped...'

'And that's why we have chocolate eggs at Easter, dad,' Daisy said. 'Isn't it?'

'That's right,' Stuart said.

'Can't we just look for the eggs now?' Dougie said.

'No,' Daisy said, 'I want to hear dad tell the Easter Story...'

Stuart carried on with the story: 'That morning, a wee little bunny was out hopping around in the early morning sunshine, and he heard a voice coming from behind this large egg-shaped rock. "Let me out!" the voice called from inside the cave. "Let me out!"'

'It was Jesus, wasn't it?' Daisy said. 'It was Jesus in the cave.'

'That's right,' Stuart said. 'So the bunny jumped against the rock. But it didn't move. He tried again and still it wouldn't budge.

'The wee little bunny looked up to the heavens and he prayed to God that he be given the strength to roll that rock away and release whoever was trapped inside.

'Then he jumped against the rock and this time the rock moved. It didn't just move. It rolled away. And Jesus appeared, and thanked the wee bunny rabbit.'

'Did that really happen, daddy?' Daisy said.

'Of course it didn't,' her brother Dougie said. 'Can we look for the eggs now?'

'Aye, go for it,' said Stuart. 'Go and get your eggies!'

Dougie and Daisy ran into the garden in their pyjamas. Dougie was ten, Daisy a couple of years younger. They both had their father's red hair.

'I can see one,' Dougie shouted, dashing across the garden to where a speck of tinfoil caught the early morning sunshine. He wiped the soil from the little egg and tucked it into his pyjama pocket and darted after another.

'I can see one too,' said Daisy, her hands in the soil.

'I've got four!' Dougie called out.

'I've got something on my hands and it smells,' Daisy said.

Theodore looked down and saw that Daisy's hands were streaked with brown.

'Looks like cat shit,' Stuart said from the patio. 'A fresh one too.'

Daisy started crying, her palms held out. 'It smells, daddy,' she said.

'Bloody cats,' Stuart said. 'Get inside and wash your hands.'

Dougie was still pocketing the little chocolate eggs. 'Silly Daisy,' he said.

Daisy ran inside, crying. 'Mummy!' she shouted. 'I've put my hand in cat poo! Mummy! Mummy!'

'Don't wake your mother,' Stuart shouted after her. 'She's having a lie-in.'

He looked up and saw Theodore peering down at him from the top of Wally's shed roof.

'Did you do that?' he said, pointing an accusing finger up at the cat.

Theodore looked down at the angry Scot. What if I did it? You don't expect me to go in my own garden? He turned his back to Stuart.

'It might have been Hamish,' Dougie said, stuffing more eggs into his bulging pyjama bottoms.

'Hamish knows not to shit in his own back garden,' Stuart said.

Exactly, thought Theodore.

Wally and Marjorie were sitting on a bench in their garden.

'When I hear the children over there, all excited, I do wonder what it would have been like...' Marjorie said, 'if we could have had some of our own.'

'Now, now,' Wally said, 'there's no point thinking like that.'

'I know,' Marjorie said. 'I just sometimes wonder...'

'No point wondering about what never happened.'

'I suppose not.'

They both drank from their mugs of tea.

'I've got something for you,' Wally said, getting up from the bench. 'For Easter.'

He crossed to his shed, and a moment later emerged carrying a large chocolate egg.

'Oh, my favourite, Wally. How did you know?'

'We have been married for nearly forty years.'

'Well, I've got something for you too.'

Marjorie got to her feet and disappeared inside the house. A minute later she returned carrying a large chocolate egg.

'Oh, my favourite, Marge! How did you know?'

'We have been married for nearly forty years.'

Theodore looked down at the old couple sitting together on their garden bench. Marjorie's face was pink in the early morning sunshine, and Wally had a glow to his cheeks, like red dabs. They each held identical chocolate eggs.

'I might have a bit of mine now,' said Marjorie.

'I might do the same,' said Wally.

Like the Stamp

Penny Black had left York and gone to study at university in Bristol. After she had graduated with a first class degree in graphic design, she had stayed on in Bristol. She got a job with a marketing agency and got engaged to Tom, who she had met on her course.

Penny had a by-line: she'd say on the phone to clients: 'It's Penny... Penny Black – like the stamp!', and people remembered it; they'd ask for her by name when they called up the agency. It was a memorable name after all. She already had a stable of half a dozen clients. Her future looked bright.

Penny was glad of the geographical as well as emotional distance that existed between her and her alcoholic of a mother and psychopath of a sister. She had managed to avoid forcing her family on Tom so far; she preferred to keep it that way.

She usually called her mother on her mobile phone every few days to make sure she was all right. When Tessa didn't answer, she began to wonder. When her mother's mobile went straight to answerphone, she began to worry. In a panic she called the landline but that too went straight to answerphone. She didn't have Ellen's mobile number. She doubted she had one.

Penny went out Saturday night to a trendy bar with Tom, but she couldn't relax, no matter how much she drank in the bar, where she sat with a group of their friends.

When they got back to their flat, they watched a programme in which young couples have to convince the viewing public that their feelings for each other are genuine, otherwise they get voted off, their 15 minutes of fame over, but Penny couldn't engage with the programme. She couldn't help but think that something terrible had happened to her mother.

Sunday morning she woke early. She got dressed, and leaving Tom sleeping, a note left on her pillow, she set off for the railway station to get the train to York.

She thought she would be back that evening. Easter Monday at the latest. She would never return.

The Great Barbecue Disaster

Emily's parents arrived shortly before midday.

Emily's father Patrick carried a large blue cool box through the kitchen and into the back garden. The cool box contained the prawns and lamb cutlets that Patrick was going to cook on the barbecue.

Patrick ordered his clothes from slim brochures that fell out of *The Times*. Theodore appraised his attire from the bottom to the top, as was his way. He eyed his well-worn suede loafers that were shiny with wear at the extremities. His trousers were flat-fronted, brick-red chinos, held up by a woven leather belt, acquired while on holiday in the north of Ibiza. His shirt was blue and white vertical stripes, which exaggerated his belly that hung over the aforementioned belt. Theodore finished his examination, noting his balding pink head that glistened with sweat.

Patrick got the barbecue out of the garage and placed it on the patio. The cool box was left in the shade cast by the garage wall.

They were waiting for the charcoal to heat up when Theodore heard a tapping from the garden behind.

There was a woman at the back door of Ellen's house. She had long, dyed-red hair and wore dark designer sunglasses and a red dress. She knocked again on the door, more loudly. 'It's Penny,' she called. 'Let me in… I know you're in there.'

Penny turned round. Theodore noticed that she was of a similar physique to her sister, Ellen. She wore bright red lipstick that matched her red dress. She paced in front of the door. She looked at her wristwatch. She looked up at the bedroom windows. The curtains were closed.

'I think something has happened to the woman who lives behind,' Jonathan told Patrick. 'Looks like her other daughter has turned up now. To see what's going on.'

'Trish said that you've been developing something of an imagination,' Patrick said. 'Well, just be careful... Dangerous things: imaginations.'

'It's not just my imagination,' Jonathan said. 'Something has happened to her, I'm sure...'

'Have I ever told you the story of the three-legged pig?' Patrick said, changing the subject.

'I don't believe so,' Jonathan said, shaking his head.

Patrick began to tell Jonathan the story of the three-legged pig: 'A man is driving down a country lane when he has a puncture. Not having a spare tyre or mobile phone, he finds a farmhouse and knocks on the farmhouse door. As the door opens, a pig runs out. The man notices that the pig only has three legs... "Why has your pig only got three legs?" he asks the farmer...'

But Jonathan was still looking over at the house behind, not really paying attention to Patrick's rambling story.

Penny Black was standing in the garden now, looking up at the bedroom windows, hands on hips. Then she disappeared down the side of the house and then Jonathan heard faint banging and knew that she was at the front door; she hadn't given up.

Jonathan turned his attention back to Patrick.

'Then the pig waited by her until the ambulance arrived,' Patrick said.

Jonathan looked round again. He couldn't see Penny. Maybe she had given up and gone home. But didn't she live in Cardiff, or some far-flung place. She wouldn't come all this way and leave again after five minutes.

He then noticed a patch of silver fur at the bottom of the hedge and realised that Theodore was also keeping an eye on the proceedings.

In the kitchen, Emily and her mum Trish were making salads to go with the lunch.

'I'm not sure I'm cut out for this,' Emily said, slicing cucumber.

'Cut out for what?' Trish said.

'You know,' Emily said, holding up the kitchen knife. 'All of this... The house, Jonathan, suburbia... Getting up at seven o'clock every morning. Going to a job I don't like. Coming home and sorting out dinner.'

'What you need to do,' Trish said, 'is to get married and have children.'

'I'm not sure I'm ready... And besides, Jonathan hasn't asked. He's never mentioned marriage...'

'Well, it was a mistake moving in together before marriage. All this try before you buy. It might be all right for cars or televisions but not when it comes to husbands.'

'What if I've made a mistake?' Emily said, putting the knife down on the chopping board.

'Everyone makes mistakes,' Trish said. 'You just have to live with them the rest of your life. That's why you should get married before you cohabit...'

'Why's dad weeing in the garden?' Emily said.

'He's always doing that,' Trish said and sighed. 'It's better than him traipsing dirt into the house every time he needs to go. Weak bladder...'

In the garden, Patrick turned from the hedge and said, 'Then the farmer said, "Well, I didn't want to eat it all at once".' He laughed until his cheeks were bright pink.

'I don't get it,' Jonathan said.

'I think it's time to put the prawns on,' Patrick said, struggling with his flies.

He bent over and retrieved a large bag of uncooked prawns from the cool box.

He had placed tin foil on the wire rack of the barbecue. He now carefully set out the prawns, fingering each one attentively.

'Five minutes!' he shouted across to the kitchen door.

Then Theodore spotted Charlie the Chihuahua. Charlie nipped through a small gap in the bottom of the hedge and made for the cool box. He placed his paws on the rim of the box that had been left open and tilted it towards him. He then launched himself upwards and into the box, ending up on top of the lamb cutlets, the lid snapping closed over him.

Patrick was bent over the barbecue, sweating fiercely. Jonathan was looking in his direction but also at the house behind. Penny was bashing on the backdoor, as hard as she could without doing it lasting damage.

After they had eaten the prawn starter, Patrick announced he would put the lamb cutlets on the barbecue before the heat from the charcoal began to die down. He flipped open the white lid of the cool box.

'Holy mackerel!' he exclaimed. 'There's a Chihuahua in the chiller!'

Jonathan got to his feet with his crutches and crossed over. 'Is it alive?' he said.

Patrick picked up the dog and held it to his chest. 'It's alive but it's chilled to the bone,' he said. 'I know... I'll warm it up a bit.'

He held the Chihuahua a couple of feet over the barbecue, so that the heat from the charcoal could warm up the frozen dog. The dog soon began to jerk back to life.

Just then Sam, who had been looking for her dog since she got up, put her head over the hedge.

She screamed. Then she shrieked, 'Steve! Steve! They're barbecuing our Charlie!'

Steve, just arrived back from his nine holes, appeared at the hedge. 'Hey! That's our dog you're cooking!'

Patrick removed the dog from over the heat and, realising what it must look like, said, 'I was just warming it up…'

'Animals!' Sam shrieked.

Charlie wriggled frantically in Patrick's hands.

Patrick dropped the dog, and Charlie dashed over to the hedge.

Moments later Sam was cradling the Chihuahua in her arms. 'Oh, Charlie,' she said, 'whatever would have happened if mummy hadn't saved you?'

Theodore watched the events from the bottom of the hedge. But then his attention was drawn by voices from behind.

Ellen had opened the backdoor, wearing a dressing gown.

'Why didn't you answer the door?' Penny said.

'I just did,' Ellen said.

'Before,' Penny said. 'I've been knocking for ages.'

'I was in the shower,' Ellen said. 'You'd better come in… What a surprise! Mum will be so pleased to see you.'

Ellen went inside and Penny followed, closing the door behind her.

'Where's mum?' Penny said.

'She's upstairs in bed,' Ellen said. 'Hardly ever leaves it… You know what she's like.'

'I'll go straight up and let her know I'm here,' Penny said.

'I'll put the kettle on,' Ellen said.

Penny went upstairs, but Ellen didn't put the kettle on. Instead she picked up the iron and stood to one side of the kitchen door.

When Penny returned moments later, she said, 'She's not there... Her bed's not been slept in. Where is she? Where's mum?'

Then Ellen cracked her over the head with the iron. Theodore blinked.

'Well, that was all a bit melodramatic,' Trish said, once the commotion over the chilled Chihuahua had died down.

'I think the lamb might be salvageable,' Patrick said, holding up a cutlet that Charlie had partly chewed before succumbing to hyperthermia and asphyxiation. 'I'll just need some scissors to trim them up a bit.'

'Well, at least no one was killed,' Trish said and laughed.

Jonathan stared at the back hedge. He had heard Penny bashing on the back door of Ellen's house. Now it was quiet. Too quiet.

Then he noticed that Theodore had gone from the bottom of the hedge. He looked around but he was nowhere to be seen.

Theodore made his way across Ellen's lawn, heading straight towards the shed.

The shed was six feet high but he managed to scrabble up one side, the side not facing the house. He pulled himself up onto the felted roof, and then inched towards the apex. He peered over the top of the shed roof.

Ellen had already removed her sister's body from the kitchen. There was just a large pool of blood and red smears across the linoleum where Penny had been dragged into the hallway behind and then up the stairs, red smudges across the beige carpet pile.

Ten minutes later, Ellen appeared. She filled a bucket with hot water at the kitchen sink and then began to wipe up the blood. She washed down the fronts of the cupboards onto which blood had splattered. She got into the cracks and crevices, wringing out her cloth into the bucket that she refilled a dozen times. Finally she took a mop and turning the radio up loud, mopped the floor with maniacal energy to Wham's *Club Tropicana*.

From time to time, Theodore glanced over at his own house. Emily, Jonathan and Trish were sitting at the patio table while Patrick was cooking the lamb chops over the barbecue, metal tongs in his right hand.

Theodore turned around. Ellen had finished in the kitchen. She had left the kitchen window and door open to dry the floor. From inside he could hear water running. She must be running a bath.

He jumped down from the shed and trotted across the lawn. He paused at the back door. Water was still running in the upstairs bathroom. He entered the kitchen.

It was only once he was halfway across the kitchen floor that he realised that he had left muddy paw prints on the linoleum. There wasn't anything he could do about it now.

He looked up at the side and spotted the little wicker basket. He jumped up and began to investigate its contents. There was a mobile phone, its screen blank, its battery no doubt dead. He pawed some pens aside but could not find what he was looking for. He furrowed his brow. The ring, Tessa's wedding ring, had gone.

He jumped down and padded into the hall.

He walked through a door into the dining room. On the dining table he noticed many beige card-backed envelopes and an album lying open. He jumped up onto the table.

The album contained stamps. Each page was a plastic envelope holding mounted sheets of stamps. There were a dozen cardboard-backed envelopes, some with names and addresses already written on in blue biro.

Then he noticed the iPad. He swiped his paw across the screen. It opened to eBay.

Ellen evidently had 98% feedback rating. Theodore looked at the items she had put up for auction.

'1841 1d Red Pl 176 NA Superb RARE PLATE with CERT Cat. £2900.00. Looking for Quick Sale'

'1840 1d Black Pl 11 JK 4m IRISH NUMERAL Matched in Red RPS Cert Cat £4730.00'

'SG. 351. N14 ½d green. "DOUBLE WATERMARK ". A very RARE superb mint'

They were all rare stamps, Theodore realised, many valued in the thousands of pounds. The auctions were due to end the next day. Ellen was set to make a small fortune.

He remembered that her father Colin had been a keen stamp collector. Ellen was selling off his collection, raising money. Money to disappear, thought Theodore. The fur along his spine began to bristle.

The running water had stopped.

He heard a door open and then steps on the upstairs landing. He jumped down from the table and trotted under the table. He saw Ellen pass in front of the dining room door. A minute later she walked past again, a pair of scissors in one hand and a carving knife in the other.

Once she had gone back upstairs, Theodore followed. He paused on the landing. He heard noises from within the bathroom. The door was pulled to but not closed. There were another three doors. Bedroom doors.

Theodore approached the back bedrooms first. He went into what had been Tessa's.

The bed was made up. The curtains were closed. There was nothing to suggest anything untoward. But a smell lingered. It was the smell of unwashed sheets, urine, sweat and perfume. The essence of Tessa Black that lingered after her death.

Then he went into Ellen's bedroom. It was very tidy: nothing out of place. A My Little Pony poster on the wall over the bed. A pink duvet pushed up against the wall. A wrinkled grey sheet. A full ashtray on the bedside table. The smell of stale cigarettes, unwashed sheets and perfume.

He jumped up onto the windowsill and slipped behind the curtains.

He looked down on his own back garden. He could see Emily, Jonathan, Trish and Patrick sitting at the patio table eating lamb cutlets and potato salad.

Theodore went into the front bedroom. This had been the master bedroom, where Colin and Tessa Black had shared the double bed, before Colin had burned to death in his shed, the fire started by a cigarette end thrown from his younger daughter's bedroom window.

On the wall facing him there was a large, framed studio photograph of Penny and Ellen, taken by Mr. Marley, the local photographer.

Penny was eight years old and Ellen five. Penny's hair was long and brown; Ellen's was short and blonde, like her mother's – before she pulled it out.

Apart from the age and hair differences, the two girls looked very similar. They had the same broad nose, brown eyes, puckered lips and slightly protruding ears.

The glass from the photo frame had shattered. Shards lay on the pink pile of the carpet at the foot of the wall, below the photograph.

A pair of short, sharp stainless steel scissors stuck out of Penny's forehead.

Theodore carefully picked his way across the pink carpet, wary of the broken glass.

He jumped up onto the salmon pink duvet, laid across the king-size bed, and then up onto the windowsill. He looked out of the window, onto the street below.

In the driveway he noticed a Ford Escort. Its tyres were completely flat, rubber black pancakes on grey concrete. The car had not been moved since Colin's death, Theodore deduced.

The toilet flushed and Theodore knew it was time to leave. He made it to the top of the stairs just as the bathroom door swung open.

He raced down the stairs, into the kitchen, skidded across the still wet floor, and out the back door into the garden. He reached the shed in the corner of the garden and scaled the side. He scrambled over the apex of the felted roof. He turned round and edged back to the ridge. He peered over.

Ellen was in the kitchen. In her hand she carried the kitchen knife, its blade coated with blood. She looked down at the paw prints on the newly washed floor. Then she approached the kitchen door. She looked out into the garden.

Dr Theodore

Theodore stayed below the ridgeline of the shed. He turned round and faced his own garden. Emily, Jonathan, Trish and Patrick were still sitting at the outside table. They were onto the dessert course.

He scaled the side of the shed and darted through the bottom of the hedge into his own garden. His intention was to alert Jonathan to the latest murder, this time sororicide.

But as he approached the table, he was grabbed up by Patrick, who had already finished his dessert.

'Ah, Theo. Where have you been? You've missed lunch!' Patrick petted him heavily. 'He's a bit matted,' he said. 'Needs a good brush.'

Theodore felt Patrick's soft belly beneath his paws. He began to knead his paws against the warm flesh. As human bellies went, it was one of the best he'd had the pleasure to work with. He began to purr.

He was just beginning to enjoy himself when he felt something move below his paws. Something that was in Patrick but not of him. He moved his paw following the gliding movement and then dabbed at it.

Patrick groaned.

'What is it, dad?' Emily said.

'Probably nothing,' Patrick said. 'Indigestion.'

'It's all the raw meat you eat,' Trish said. 'Steak Tartare for breakfast. That can't be good for you.'

'That's only on a Saturday,' Patrick said. 'A little treat.'

He groaned again as Theodore pushed in his other paw, trying to trap the movement inside him.

Theodore closed his eyes, deep in thought.

It was a beef tapeworm of the species *taenia saginata*. It had been inside Patrick for almost two years, now ten feet long.

'I think that's enough of your prodding,' Patrick said. He picked Theodore up and placed him on the ground before the cat could complete his diagnosis.

'Maybe you should get it checked out,' Emily said.

'I'm sure it's nothing,' Patrick said, his own hand on his side and a note of uncertainty to his voice.

'Please, dad,' Emily said. 'For me, if not for you.'

'You have been complaining of stomach pains,' Trish said.

'Yes, all right then. I'll make an appointment on Tuesday.'

Theodore examined the floor for any food dropped from the table. He then remembered that he had been about to alert Jonathan to the latest murder before he had been grabbed up by Patrick. He approached Jonathan's feet and miaowed.

Jonathan had already managed to manoeuvre the conversation back to his murderous neighbour. By the animation in his voice, Theodore understood that he had had more than a couple of glasses of wine. 'She's killed her mum, I swear... And now she's probably about to kill her sister.'

You're behind the times, thought Theodore.

'Well, at least it has stayed fine,' Trish said.

'Yes, it's been a lovely afternoon,' Patrick said. 'Just a shame about that little dog getting stuck in the cool box.'

'Well, never mind about that,' Trish said. 'There was no harm done.'

'A killer in the house behind,' Jonathan said, slurring slightly, 'and not one of you cares. She even killed a Shih Zhu and then a guide dog...'

'Talking of dogs, what do you get if you cross a bulldog with a Shih Zhu?' Patrick said.

'It's no joking matter,' Jonathan said. 'She's a homicidal maniac. A killer... A psychotic killer!'

Emily slammed her wine glass down on the table, causing a crack from stem to lip. 'Will you just shut up?' she said, staring at Jonathan. 'I've had enough. Enough!'

Jonathan shook his head. He didn't say anything.

Patrick filled the gap. 'Bullshit,' he said. 'It's a bullshit. Get it? A bull dog and a Shih Zhu...'

Nobody laughed.

'Maybe it's time we were going,' Trish said. 'Leave these two to it.'

'Yes,' said Patrick, gazing at the two empty bottles of Chardonnay on the table. 'We'd better be getting back to Acaster Mildew.'

Theodore Plays God

After the barbecue had been cleared away and the washing up done, Theodore turned his attention back to Ellen. He took up position on the shed in her garden. He watched as Ellen poured come clear liquid from a bottle into a glass. She downed it and winced.

Theodore looked over at Geoffrey's bungalow.

Geoffrey was in the kitchen. He was going through his cupboards, his hands grasping at small packets and packages.

Theodore watched as Geoffrey began to pop tablets from plastic containers into a bowl, his hands shaking. When the bowl was half full of tablets, he poured a glass of water and then carried the bowl and the glass into the conservatory. He sat down at the table, the bowl and glass in front of him.

He removed his dark glasses. His milky white eyes were red rimmed. He picked a couple of pills from the bowl and washed them down with a mouthful of water. He took another handful and swallowed them too.

Theodore jumped down from the shed roof and darted through the gap in the bottom of the hedge that Lucy had made. He approached the glass doors of the conservatory.

Inside Geoffrey swilled down another couple of tablets. Then he wiped tears from his eyes before reaching for more.

Theodore scraped his claws against the glass.

Geoffrey didn't hear. He took another handful of pills and swallowed them.

Theodore scratched again against the glass.

Geoffrey turned to the doors. 'Lucy?' he said. He got to his feet. He crossed to the conservatory doors. He slid open the doors.

Theodore slipped through the opening. He jumped up onto the table.

Geoffrey was still standing at the conservatory doors. 'Lucy!' he called out to the garden. 'Is that you Lucy?'

Then Theodore knocked the bowl of pills to the floor. The bowl smashed and the pills were scattered across the floor.

Geoffrey turned. 'What's going on?'

He staggered back to the table. He felt across the surface to where the bowl of pills had been.

Theodore jumped soundlessly to the floor.

Geoffrey got down on his hands and knees. He knelt on the floor; then placed the palms of his hands together. He looked up to the ceiling, his milky eyes filled with tears, and said, 'If it be your will…'

Theodore jumped up onto the kitchen side. He looked at the empty packets of pills and wondered if it were possible to overdose on multivitamins and cod liver oil capsules. He jumped down and a moment later exited through the conservatory doors.

He glanced behind him. Geoffrey was still on his knees, still gazing up at the ceiling, his hands placed together in prayer.

Emily Packs Her Bags

The French windows were open when Theodore got back home. He wandered into the lounge.

Jonathan was on the sofa, watching *The Birds* on the television. Theodore jumped up onto the cushion next to him.

Jonathan paused the film. 'You believe me, don't you?' he said.

Theodore purred back reassuringly.

'She's a murderer,' Jonathan said.

Theodore purred his agreement.

'We just need to prove it,' Jonathan said. 'We need proof. Then we call the police and they can deal with her.'

Proof, thought Theodore; he needed to find Tessa's wedding ring. But if it wasn't in the house behind, where was it?

Theodore went upstairs to look for Emily. She was in the bedroom, sorting out clothes.

Theodore jumped up onto the front windowsill.

In the fading light, he saw Linda exit the side door of her house. In her hands she carried a jam jar of brushes, another jam jar of water, a box of acrylic paints and a palette.

Linda crouched down by the side of Steve's white Audi. The car was again parked on the verge in front of her house. Dead daffodils lay flattened beneath its tyres.

She squeezed a dollop of green acrylic onto her palette and licked the end of her paint brush.

This is going to be interesting, thought Theodore.

He turned his attention back to Emily.

She had a small suitcase open on the bed and was pushing her clothes into it.

'Guess we'll be travelling light,' she said. She looked over at Theodore. Her eyes were red from crying.

Theodore jumped down from the windowsill and then up onto the bed. He let Emily pick him up and hold him to her chest.

'This house,' Emily said. 'It's like a private trap... It holds us in like a prison. You know what I think? I think that we're all in our private traps, clamped in them, and none of us can ever get out. We scratch and we claw, but only at the air, only at each other, and for all of it, we never budge an inch.'

Clap trap, Theodore thought; a house is what you make of it. He was reminded of the sign hung on the vestibule door: *A House is Not A Home Without a Cat.* He was a cat. This was a house. It was their home. It was as simple as that.

Emily said, 'It's a trap... A trap of our own making. We have to get out while we can.'

You cannot run from yourself, thought Theodore.

'I just can't live like this,' Emily said. 'I can't go on like this... pretending everything's fine. Pretending this is me. I'm not happy. I need to do something about it.'

She put Theodore back down on the bed. She crossed to the bedside cabinet and took out the rolls of bank notes wrapped in clear plastic from the drawer. She pushed the money into the suitcase and then closed the lid.

'That should last a few months,' she said.

She was pacing in front of the bedroom window and gesturing at the houses and gardens of suburbia.

136

'I should never have come here. This isn't the life that I want.'

She put the suitcase into the bottom of the wardrobe and closed the door. 'Tomorrow our new life begins,' she said.

Dance How You Like!

Emily woke early on Easter Monday. She sat up in bed and remembered that today she was going to escape this suburban nightmare and begin the rest of her life. She looked across the bedroom at the wardrobe, where her case waited. She glanced at the drawer of her bedside table, where she had stashed the shop's takings. She stared up at the bedroom ceiling. She would just have to choose her moment to slip out and take Theodore with her; she didn't want Jonathan making a scene.

Theodore was sleeping on the bed beside her. She stroked him for some minutes.

When she got up she parted the curtains. The front window faced east, towards York. She could make out the Minster in the distance. In the middle ground, there were some blocks of flats and an ugly concrete water tower on stilts. On the side of the water tower somebody had painted in large red letters: 'VOYER!'

'She still can't spell,' Emily said to herself.

Theodore jumped up onto the windowsill. His attention was drawn by a commotion in the street below.

Steve was standing in front of his car, parked on Linda's front verge.

'Did you do this?' he demanded of Linda.

Linda was dressed in her purple jogging gear. 'I don't know what you're talking about,' she said with a misplaced grin.

'My car,' Steve said. 'Someone has painted flowers and trees on it... It's a bloody woodland scene!'

'I can see,' Linda said. 'How pretty!'

'This will cost a fortune to sort.'

'You could always leave it as it is. It's a big improvement.'

'It's going to need respraying.'

'Well, I need to get going. Can't stand here chatting...'

'You did it, didn't you?' Steve said.

'It's Dance How You Like this morning,' Linda said.

'You're going to pay for this...'

'You should try it! Unlock some of that aggression.'

'I would be calm if you hadn't done this to my car.'

'Don't want to be late,' Linda said and began walking away, a skip in her step, leaving Steve to contemplate his paintwork.

Emily pulled the curtains closed. 'See what I mean,' she said. 'Suburbia! Get me out of here!'

The Origins of Marmalade

Theodore went into the back bedroom. It was still full of unpacked boxes. He jumped up onto the windowsill.

Wally and Stuart were arguing over the hedge. Theodore soon picked up the thread of their argument. It was over the origins of marmalade.

'It's as English as tea,' Wally shouted at his neighbour.

'It's Scottish, I tell you,' Stuart said. 'Queen Mary brought it back to Scotland. She had sea sickness and they gave her marmalade to settle her stomach. And she took a taste to it and had it brought over to Scotland in the middle of the sixteenth century.'

'I've never heard so much rubbish,' Wally said. 'It was Henry the Eighth who brought it over. Before Mary had a dodgy tummy, we were already enjoying marmalade on our toast. You Scots are always one step behind.'

'Och, och, bollocks,' Stuart said. 'You might have had a bit of some shredless jelly, but it was Janet Keiller of Dundee who added the peel to it. Her husband bought the oranges at the harbourside and she shredded the peel and boiled down the oranges to make the marmalade that we know today. They were doing that in the seventeen hundreds. What you English were scoffing back then was flavoured jelly. Not proper marmalade.'

'Absolute nonsense,' Wally said. 'Shakespeare was eating marmalade on his toast before your Janet

Keiller's great grandmother was even born. Not just oranges but quinces and all sorts of fruit.'

Stuart rolled up his shirt sleeves and squared up to the hedge. 'It's Scottish,' he said. 'You never thought of putting the shred in it. That's what we Scots did. We put in the shred. Without the shred, it's not marmalade!'

'Well, it is marmalade,' Wally said. 'Just shredless.'

'Like this country,' Stuart said. 'Shredless.'

'Some people like their marmalade without the shred,' said Wally.

'Just you wait,' Stuart said, 'Us Scots will have our independence. Then Trevor Trout won't put up with your nonsense no more. We won't put up with your shredless marmalade!'

Trevor Trout was the then leader of the Scottish Nationalist Party. He carried on the tradition of leaders of the Scottish Nationalist Party being named after fish.

'Your Trevor Trout will not outlaw our shredless marmalade…'

'You prick!' shouted Stuart, escalating the argument a notch.

'Talking of pricks,' Wally said, 'you want to be careful where you go putting yours.'

'What do you mean by that?'

'Ellen Black,' Wally said. 'I know what you've been up to… Carrying on with a girl half your age… You should bloody know better.'

'What was that?'

Both men turned. Leslie was standing several yards behind Stuart, her dressing gown pulled tightly around her.

'Who's been putting their prick where?'

'I'd better get on,' Walter said. He adjusted his cap; then made for the safety of his shed.

Stuart stared at his wife. He had some explaining to do.

However, the ensuing argument escalated and less than an hour later, Stuart was in his car, Hamish in his cat carrier in the passenger seat, on their way back to Scotland.

Well at least Hamish is out of the way, thought Theodore, looking down on the scene from the bedroom window.

The Evidence

A magpie swooped down and picked up a scrap of silver from the lawn. Theodore realised that it was a fragment of tinfoil, a remnant of yesterday's barbecue. He watched as the bird disappeared into the white blossom of the apple tree in the corner of Geoffrey's garden.

Theodore thought of the basket in the kitchen of Ellen's house. The wedding ring that was no longer there. He remembered the flash of black and white feathers coming out of the kitchen.

He looked again at the apple tree and miaowed.

He trotted downstairs and miaowed at the French windows until Jonathan opened them.

He trotted across the lawn, through the hedge, and cut across Ellen's lawn. He entered Geoffrey's garden and made for the apple tree.

He ascended the four feet of near vertical trunk and gained the V of two branches. He looked up and sighted the magpies' nest up one of the branches. He climbed the branch. As he reached the nest, the branch bowed under his weight. He peered inside.

There were several scraps of tinfoil, and there in the middle was the gold ring set with diamonds. He took hold of the ring with his teeth and was about to turn around when the pair of magpies attacked.

They flew at him, pecking at his face, his body. They were everywhere. He looked down at the lawn, ten feet below. Then he dropped from the branch.

He landed but swallowed the ring on impact. He got to his feet. The magpies swooped down and pecked at his body, their sharp beaks finding their way through his long fur and piercing his flesh.

He scrambled back through the bottom of the hedge still pursued by the birds, the ring lodged in his throat.

Jonathan had suffered vertigo for as long as he could remember. It was an affliction he had learned to live with, but the condition had affected his life to the detriment.

His final year of university, he had been sent into the field to log a previously unmapped mountainside in Wales. While he had spluttered some protests, his tutor had assured him he would be fine. 'It's all in the mind,' he'd been told.

He had restricted his mapping to the lower reaches of the mountain, and on his return his tutor had given him a very low grade, resulting in him scraping a 2:2 in his degree, which meant that he was out of the running for a lot of jobs with the larger consultancies. When he was offered a job by a small consultancy on the outskirts of Leeds, he jumped at the opportunity.

He tried to explain to people that vertigo was not a fear of heights, as a lot of people seemed to believe, but an actual physical reaction to being up high.

He had placed *Vertigo* at the bottom of the pile of Hitchcock DVDs he was working his way through. He had now reached the bottom of the pile. He bent down and was about to put the DVD into the machine when Theodore appeared in front of the French windows, miaowing to be let back in.

Jonathan crossed to the windows and opened them. The cat stayed where it was. 'Please yourself,' he said.

Theodore miaowed up at him, a strange, raspy miaow, as though he had something stuck in his throat.

He placed his head near the ground and began to heave.

Soon he had thrown up what looked like a short length of twisted grey rope.

Jonathan looked at the knot of cat fur and winced. 'Nice,' he said.

Then he noticed something glisten from within the salivary fur. He reached over and picked up the fur ball and peeling it apart, removed a gold ring, set with diamonds.

'A wedding ring…' he murmured. 'Where did you get this?'

Theodore looked back over the garden, towards the house behind.

'It's hers, isn't it?' Jonathan said. 'It's Tessa Black's wedding ring, isn't it?'

Theodore stared up at him and blinked yes.

'This is the proof we need,' Jonathan said. 'I think it's time we confronted Ellen.'

He made his way across the garden to the back hedge, Theodore following behind.

The Vertigo DVD was left on the floor in front of the television.

There was a green wheelie bin pulled in front of the back door. He could see Ellen inside the kitchen.

'Hey!' Jonathan shouted over at her. 'Can I have a word?'

Ellen pushed the wheelie bin aside and walked across to the boundary hedge. 'Yes, what is it?'

Jonathan held the wedding ring up. 'Do you know what this is?'

'Yes,' Ellen said, 'it's my mum's wedding ring. Where did you get it?'

'It's proof,' Jonathan said. 'Proof that you killed her.'

'Give it to me,' Ellen snapped.

'No. This ring is the proof! You killed your mum. Then you killed her dog. And now you've killed your sister.'

'Penny?'

'Yes. She came yesterday. I saw her... She knew something was up. Then you killed her too. Didn't you?'

Ellen folded her arms across her chest; she was wearing another of her father's old shirts. She stared at Jonathan a moment; then said flatly: 'My mum's in bed and Penny's upstairs having a shower.'

'I don't believe you,' Jonathan said.

'See for yourself.'

He looked at the hedge. He could hardly jump over it on his crutches. 'Well, that's not really possible.'

'You'll have to walk round,' Ellen said.

'It might take me a while.'

'I'm not going anywhere.'

Jonathan noticed Theodore entering the bottom of the hedge. The cat miaowed. 'I'll walk round then,' he said. 'But if they aren't there, I'm going to call the police.'

'They are both here,' Ellen said. 'I think you've got a screw loose... You think I've been murdering my family? You're the bloody psycho!' She laughed in his face.

'Five minutes,' Jonathan said, turning red in the face. 'Five minutes and we'll see who's the psycho!'

Ellen had already turned and was walking back to the house. The door was slammed shut behind her.

Jonathan turned and began to walk back across his own overgrown garden. Theodore made his way towards Ellen's back door.

As The Crow Flies

Jonathan grabbed his mobile phone from the side. From upstairs he heard water running. 'I'm going out,' he shouted. 'I'm going to prove that I'm not imaging things…'

'Whatever,' Emily shouted down.

As soon as Jonathan had shut the front door behind him, Emily turned off the bath taps and called a taxi.

'As soon as possible,' she said into her mobile. Then: 'Twenty minutes? That's fine… I'll be waiting.'

She heard the front door open and close. She peaked through the bedroom curtains and saw Jonathan begin to make his way round to Ellen's house. It will take him at least fifteen minutes to get there and another fifteen minutes to make his way back. She had at least half an hour to get away. She just had to find Theodore and get him in the cat box.

Although Jonathan had only seen Penny at a distance over the hedge yesterday, he recognised her straightaway. She was wearing the same designer sunglasses even though it was overcast. He also noticed that her dyed red hair was still wet. So she had been having a shower, Jonathan reasoned. Ellen wasn't lying about that.

'Where's Ellen?' Jonathan asked.

'She just went out,' Penny said.

'Where?' Jonathan said, 'I need to speak to her.'

'She was acting strange,' Penny said. 'We argued and she left.'

147

'Where to?'

'I think she's gone to the church,' Penny said. 'It's where dad is buried. It's where she goes when she's upset. I was about to go after her... But, as you can see, I wasn't dressed. I'd just got out of the shower. I'm going to look for her.'

Penny shut the front door and began to walk away down the street.

'I'll come with you,' Jonathan said.

But Penny was already striding down the street.

Jonathan set off after her on his crutches but he soon lagged behind. He watched as she turned right at the top of the street.

He rested on his crutches for a few seconds. He took his mobile phone from his dressing gown pocket. He called Emily's mobile but she didn't answer. He sent a text. 'Come to church. I was right about Ellen. I'm onto her.'

Theodore rested below a parked car. He knew that it couldn't be Penny that Jonathan was following: she was dead. He had seen Ellen whack her over the head with the iron. It was Ellen they were following. Ellen wearing Penny's sunglasses, dress and hair.

When Jonathan set off again on his crutches, Theodore followed him, darting from car to car until he turned right onto York Road.

He waited until Jonathan was twenty yards further up Constantine Crescent before he turned the corner.

He had to pause as a taxi entered the other end of the crescent. On the side of the taxi was written Crow-Line Taxis. Theodore watched as the taxi came to a stop in front of his house. The driver beeped his horn.

A few seconds later Emily appeared, dragging behind her a suitcase on wheels. Theodore padded behind a tree. He watched as the driver got out and put the case in the boot. Emily was looking up and down the street. She called Theodore's name. She disappeared back inside the house. She came out again. She called his name again.

When he peered around the tree, he saw that Emily was standing on the footpath, holding a cat carrier. He looked across the road, in the direction that Jonathan had taken. He was nowhere to be seen.

But Theodore knew where he was going and he knew that the quickest way to get there was as the crow flies. He spied the church steeple in the distance.

He peered back down the street. Emily was standing by the side of the taxi, her head bent down, talking to the driver.

Theodore chose the moment to dart across the road and then, rather than following Jonathan along York Road, he nipped under a gate, along the side of a bungalow and dashed across a lawn.

A dog barked and set off after him but Theodore was already at the hedge; then through it and into another garden.

'I can't leave without my cat,' Emily explained to the taxi driver. 'Give me a few minutes and I'll go and look for him.'

Emily headed back inside the house. Once back inside the front door, she noticed the sign that hung from the vestibule door.

She called Theodore's name. She knew he wasn't going to come, even if he heard her. It was as if he knew.

She took her mobile from her pocket and read the text from Jonathan. 'Come to church. I was right about Ellen. I'm onto her.'

Outside the taxi driver beeped his horn.

Vertigo

*"St Stephen, York Road, Acomb. 1834 by G. T.
Andrews; the chancel 1851, perhaps by J. A. Hansom. w tower
with broach-spire. Lancet windows. No aisles, but transepts."*
Sir Nikolaus Pevsner, *The Buildings of England
Yorkshire: York & The East Riding*

Theodore climbed to the top of the church wall and surveyed the churchyard.

Then he jumped down and picked his way between the headstones. Between the trees he saw a flash of red. Ellen was making her way towards the entrance of the church. Theodore crouched down in front of a sign. It was a laminated sheet of A4 paper. It read:

THIS MONUMENT
MARKS THE GRAVE
OF
EDWARD TENNYSON
(1813-1890)

EDWARD WAS THE YOUNGER
BROTHER OF THE POET ALFRED LORD
TENNYSON AND SPENT THE LAST 58
YEARS OF HIS LIFE IN AN ACOMB
ASYLUM

Theodore looked at Edward Tennyson's tomb. A crucifix adorned the grey stone. Over the years the heavy tomb had sunk into the soil. If its significance hadn't been known, the stone box would have been overgrown years ago.

Theodore creased his brow and wondered at the fragile line that separated creative genius and insanity. It was better not to think too much; nothing good could come of it. He blinked his eyes.

He looked across at the church. He got to his paws and made his way towards the church. He paused beneath the giant beech tree. There was a path that led down to Acomb Green. He watched as Jonathan appeared at the church gate. He opened it and entered the church yard. A crutch below each shoulder, he made his way up the path, swinging his broken foot in its plastic boot in front of him.

As he neared, Theodore shot out from his hiding spot and crossed to the church door, making sure that Jonathan saw him.

Jonathan followed after the cat. He hesitated in the doorway; then walked inside.

The church was empty. He called quietly for Theodore but the cat was nowhere to be seen. He recalled from his Pevsner's guide that the church didn't have an aisle but only transepts and the tower was on the western side.

If Penny had come inside the church, she must be hiding, he thought. He made his way along the western transept, glancing from left to right, down each pew, to make sure she wasn't hiding in a pew.

He reached the altar, where two big brass candlesticks stood. He walked around it and then looked back along the transept. He was about to give up when he heard a faint miaow nearby. He looked to his right and noticed a small door. He walked over and pushed the door open.

There were spiral stone steps leading up the western tower. He heard a miaow from overhead.

He took a deep breath and began to climb the tower steps.

As he went up, he began to feel dizzy and sweat beaded on his forehead. He focussed on placing his crutches and his left foot squarely on each step. Sweat stung his eyes and he blinked to clear them.

Ahead he heard Theodore miaow loudly, like he was being held against his will and trying to get away.

He took another step and his head was at the same level as the belfry floor. Then he made the mistake of looking down. He placed a hand to his forehead and dropped his crutch. The crutch found its way back down the stairs, clattering to a stop on the stone floor.

He looked up and saw Penny, or who he thought was Penny. She towered over him. She was holding Theodore, one hand around his throat, the other gripping his body.

'He brought you to me,' she said and laughed. 'What a clever little boy!'

She dropped Theodore onto the floor where he scrambled away.

'You're not Penny are you?' Jonathan said.

She removed her red hair, revealing her own blonde hair that she'd tied back. It was Ellen, Jonathan realised.

'You killed Penny, didn't you?'

Ellen smiled. 'You know I did,' she said. 'Like you know that I killed my mum and the dog. Two dogs actually. Oh, and my dad… but that one *was* an accident, so it doesn't really count, does it?'

Jonathan took a step upwards to try to get on the same level as Ellen. But Ellen took the opportunity to kick the other crutch away from under his arm. It clattered down the stairwell to join its partner.

Jonathan took another step upwards placing his weight momentarily on his bad foot. He winced with pain and Ellen kicked him in the shoulder.

'I think this is the end for you,' Ellen said.

'No!' Jonathan shouted.

She raised her foot in the air, ready to kick him again.

Theodore chose his moment. He rushed at her other leg, throwing his whole weight against it.

Ellen lost her balance. She screamed as she fell onto Jonathan. She grabbed him and they both fell down the stairwell together.

Theodore approached the edge and peered down. He had a good head for heights: he was a cat after all.

Jonathan groaned in pain where he lay. He tried to move but was pinned to the ground by Ellen. She was lying on top of him, her chest over his stomach, her head on his chest. He squirmed below her but couldn't get out from under her.

Then Ellen raised her head from his chest and looked him in the face. 'That bloody cat,' she said smiling madly. 'He's going to get it once I've finished with you...' She got to her feet and staggered towards the altar.

Jonathan got into a crouch but couldn't get to his feet: he had broken his other foot.

Ellen soon returned. She was holding a big brass candlestick in her right hand. She did a few practice strokes as she approached Jonathan, who was now on all fours, trying to crawl away.

She held the candlestick in the air, ready to bash Jonathan over the back of the head.

Then Theodore dropped from the belfry, his claws out. He landed on Ellen's head and dug his claws in.

Ellen screamed and dropped the candlestick. She raised her hands and pulled the cat off her head and threw him to the floor.

Ellen picked up the candlestick again and went after the cat. She cornered him behind the altar.

Theodore cowered.

'You are going to regret ever setting eyes on me,' Ellen said.

She held up the candlestick, ready to strike.

Theodore closed his eyes and tensed his body.

He felt a warm liquid splash over him; it was not what he had expected death to be like.

He opened his eyes. Emily was standing in front of him, the other candlestick in her hands. She dropped it to the floor.

Ellen lay on the floor beside him. She was dead. He realised that the warm splash was blood. Her blood.

Theodore inspected his fur. It was coated with red. For Bastet's sake, he swore.

He turned his attention back to Ellen. He noticed that tranquillity had descended across her face. In death she had found peace.

Welcome Back to God's Own County

Ellen takes a last drag on the cigarette and drops it from her bedroom window, down the gap between the house and the shed, like she has done a thousand times or more, but this time, rather than smouldering out with the rest of the butts, the shed explodes with a bang.

Her dad Colin staggers out. He's on fire. He stands in the middle of the lawn. He flaps his hands against his clothes, trying to put out the flames. He turns and faces the back of his house. He looks up at her bedroom window. 'Hell,' he shouts. 'Hell fire!'

Ellen is 14 years old. She has unicorns and princesses on her curtains, pink and blue. She has grown out of them but her dad has promised her new curtains, yellow ones. She wonders if she'll get the yellow curtains now.

From the bedroom next to hers, she hears Penny scream. She is three years older, about to go off to university.

Then she sees her mum run outside, wet tea towels in her hands. 'Get down on the lawn,' Tessa shouts at her dad.

Her dad lies down on the lawn and her mum pushes the wet tea towels against the flames and smouldering clothing. Her dad has stopped screaming and she knows he is dead. His mouth is open; his gums peeled back to show off his yellow teeth.

There is a corpse, with blackened, blistered skin, clothes burnt onto flesh, lying in the middle of a neatly trimmed lawn.

Her mum shakes out one of the tea towels. It is streaked with soot. She lays it over her dad's face.

The tea towel has rolling green hills and winding blue streams on it, and bares the slogan: 'Welcome to God's Own County'.

Ellen stares down at her dad. She is too shocked to speak. Her mum is kneeling by the corpse.

Then Tessa gets slowly to her feet and turns to face the house. Her eyes are red rimmed from smoke and tears. Her eyebrows are singed off. She has black smudges across her face and clothes.

She points a finger up at Ellen, still standing in the window. 'You!' she screams. 'You've killed him... It's your fault... It's all your fault!'

Emily bent down and closed Ellen's eyelids.

'What have I done?' she said. 'I didn't mean to kill her.'

'Can you call an ambulance?' Jonathan said, crawling across the floor towards them. 'I think I've gone and broken my other foot.'

'I told you not to get messed up in other people's business,' Emily said.

'Please,' Jonathan whimpered, 'call an ambulance.'

'You stay there,' Emily said, her mobile phone in her hand. 'I can't get a signal in here.'

Theodore approached Emily and miaowed.

Emily looked down at him. 'And you're having a bath when we get home.'

Home, thought Theodore.

'Yes, home,' Emily said and began to make for the doors.

And Theodore followed her out of the church.

Stuart Turns a Corner

Wally was prodding at a fire with a stick. There was not even a whisper of smoke; the fire had gone out long ago.

Marjorie came over. 'What's got into you? Moping about...'

'I'm going to miss him.'

'Well, it was your big mouth that got him into trouble, you great big turnip.'

'I know that,' Walter said. 'I should have held my tongue.'

'You were always arguing, winding each other up.'

'I know that,' Walter said. 'But we got on all right, all said and done. Now I won't have anyone to talk to.'

'Well you should have thought about that before you put your great big foot in it,' Marjorie said.

Walter didn't reply.

'How about I get you a nice slice of quiche.' Marjorie said. 'That'll cheer you up.'

'What type of quiche have we got?'

'How about tunkey? I think I've got some in the cupboard...'

'Tuna and turkey? One of my favourites...' he said with the beginnings of a smile on his lips.

'I'll go and fetch you a slice, Marjorie said. 'And I'm sure that Stuart will be back.'

'How do you know?'

'Call it woman's intuition. He'll be back with his tail between his legs. Mark my words.'

Stuart made it as far as Scotch Corner services before he began to have misgivings.

As he dunked his shortbread in his cup of service station coffee, he thought of Dougie and Daisy. A tear came to his eye. He lifted his shortbread from the waxed paper cup. Half of it was left in his coffee. 'Sod it,' he said. He sat bleary-eyed for a few minutes more.

Then he took his mobile phone from his shirt pocket and began to write a message, an ode to his wife. He would win Leslie back with his words:

> Oh my love is like a big thistle
> From you I'll never part
> Oh my love is like a great missile
> That's aimed straight for your heart
>
> I could never leave you, darling
> I hope you understand
> And I will love you always dear
> I'll always be your man
>
> I'll always be your man, my dear
> No matter where you are
> I am returning to your heart
> I'm turning round this car

He pressed send and then drained his coffee.

Hamish was still in his cat carrier, strapped into the passenger seat beside him. Stuart opened up the front of the carrier and took his cat out. 'I've got a treat for you, Hamish,' he said.

He took a little plastic container of milk he had swiped from Burger King and peeled the top off.

As Hamish lapped up the milk, Stuart said, 'We're going home!'

Why Patrick Only Has Three Fingers

'Who knows how long that thing had been living in him?' Trish said.

'Well, it's gone now,' Emily said. 'That's the main thing.'

'A tapeworm? I mean how disgusting is that? I'm doing all the cooking from now. No more Steak Tartare for him. Everything's going to be well done from now on.'

'How did they get rid of it?'

'They gave him two tablets,' Trish said. 'He was two hours on the toilet… It's a wonder it didn't break in two.'

'That's a lot of number twos,' Emily said.

Trish was thoughtful for a moment; then said, 'It's always good to have a good clear out from time to time.'

Patrick was kneeling in front of the backdoor. He had drilled four holes, one in each corner where the cat flap was going to go. He took out the jigsaw and cut lines through the door between the holes. Once he had removed the rectangle of wood, he tried to fit the cat flap in the gap but it wouldn't fit.

'What's up?' Jonathan asked. He was sitting at the outside table in a wheelchair, both his feet clad in grey plastic boots.

'I think we just need to straighten up this side,' Patrick said. 'It's not straight.'

He picked up the jigsaw again and cut into the side.

There was a bang inside as the vestibule door was blown shut. Patrick lurched forward and the blade of the jigsaw chopped through the forefinger of his left hand. The finger flew up into the air in a spray of blood.

Theodore was also supervising the fitting of the cat flap from the edge of the lawn. He watched as the finger landed in front of him.

He wasn't the only animal to see it.

Charlie the Chihuahua had his head poking through the bottom of the hedge. Charlie darted forwards, past Theodore and was on the finger. Theodore got to his feet as Charlie dashed back past him, Patrick's finger gripped in his little jaws. Theodore turned and gave chase.

'I've lost my finger,' Patrick said, his hand in the air, blood running down his arm.

'Well, where is it?' Trish said.

'That little dog ran off with it. The one I shut in the cool box.'

'Well, that'll teach you a lesson,' Trish said. 'Payback... You shouldn't have shut it in the cool box.'

'That was an accident.'

'I could say the same about your finger.'

Just then Theodore appeared back on the lawn. In his mouth he held Patrick's finger, now with little rows of teeth marks in it. Theodore dropped the bloody morsel at Patrick's feet with a short miaow.

'Look, Theo's brought it back,' Emily said. 'Well done Theo! What a clever cat!'

'Quick!' Patrick said. 'Get some frozen peas!'

'I don't think we have frozen peas,' Emily said, opening the freezer door. 'Will sweetcorn do?'

'Whatever,' Patrick said. 'Just be quick about it. I want my finger back...'

'Oh, stop flapping,' Trish said. 'They'll soon sew it back on...'

Emily looked doubtfully at the badly mauled finger, before popping it into the bag of sweetcorn.

'You'll have to drive,' Patrick said to Trish, taking the bag of sweetcorn from his daughter.

'Well, don't go bleeding over the seat,' Trish said. 'We don't want blood on the upholstery.

After Trish and Patrick had made a hasty departure to York Hospital, Emily inspected her father's handiwork.

'He's left the job half done and his tools lying around. Can you finish it?'

Jonathan wheeled himself over. 'I can try,' he said.

And Theodore sloped off into the garden.

He jumped up onto the roof of Wally's shed. Wally was bent over a fire in the corner, prodding at the embers with a stick.

'You're never going to get that going,' Stuart said from the other side of the hedge. 'Not with all that there prodding you're doing...'

'What do you know about fires?' Wally said.

'I'll tell you what I know about starting fires,' Stuart said. 'Us Scots have been starting fires since you English knew how to suck on your mother's teat.'

'Get away with you!' said Wally.

Marjorie then appeared behind the two men. 'I've made you a special quiche,' she said.

In her hands she carried a plate, the quiche already cut into triangles. 'I made it for you both to share.'

'What kind of quiche is it?' Wally said.

'It's haggis and turnip,' Marjorie said. 'To celebrate Stuart's return and to make amends for your big mouth...'

'Haggis and neeps,' Stuart said, clapping his hands together. 'You'd better pass me a slice over.'

'Don't you be taking the big bit,' Wally said.

As the English and the Scots made friends again over quiche, Theodore heard a scratting coming from Geoffrey's bungalow. He looked across and saw a young Golden Retriever at the doors of the conservatory.

A few moments later, the doors slid open and the young dog bounced out onto the lawn.

'There you go, Sasha,' Geoffrey said. 'You have a run about.'

Theodore turned to the house behind.

It was boarded up; its former occupants, a whole family, all dead.

The police had recovered Penny Black's scalped corpse from the bath. Then they had dug up Tessa Black's body from her husband's grave. The autopsy confirmed that she had died from a massive brain haemorrhage.

Theodore remembered her screaming, 'Going to the dogs,' and then the silence from the house that followed as Ellen pulled the curtains across.

He closed his eyes. Better not to think too much, he thought, and settled down for a nap.

April 2013 – February 2018

A Note on the Author

The author lives in a house surrounded by very high hedges.

THE FIRST OF NINE

The Case of the Clementhorpe Killer

by

James Barrie

When Theodore discovers his neighbour Peter Morris with his head bashed in, he sets out on the trail of the Clementhorpe Killer.

Set among the back alleys of York, *The First of Nine* is murder mystery with a feline twist. It is Theodore's first foray into crime detection. It is the first of his nine lives...